PRAISE FOR JENNI JAMES

Beauty and the Beast
(Faerie Tale Collection)

"Jenni James takes this well loved faerie tale and gives it a paranormal twist. Very well written and hard to put down, even on my cruise vacation where I had plenty to do. Looking forward to others in Jenni's Faerie Tale series. A great escape!"

—Amazon reviewer, 5-star review

Pride & Popularity
(The Jane Austen Diaries)

"This book was unputdownable. I highly recommend it to any fan of Jane Austen, young or old. Impatiently awaiting the rest of the series."

*—Jenny Ellis, Librarian and
Jane Austen Society of North America*

"Having read several other Young Adult retellings of Pride and Prejudice - I must admit that Pride and Popularity by Jenni James is my top choice and receives my highest recommendation! In my opinion, it is the most plausible, accessible, and well-crafted YA version of Pride and Prejudice I have read! I can hardly wait to read the [next] installment in this series!"

—*Meredith, Austenesque Reviews*

"I started reading Pride and Popularity and couldn't put it down! I stayed up until 1:30 in the morning to finish. I've never been happier to lose sleep. I was still happy this morning. You can't help but be happy when reading this feel good book. Thank you Jenni for the fun night!"

—*Clean Teen Fiction*

Northanger Alibi
(The Jane Austen Diaries)

"Twilight obsessed teens (and their moms) will relate to Claire's longing for the fantastical but will be surprised when they find the hero is even better than a vampire or werewolf. Hilarious, fun and romantic!"

—*TwilightMOMS.com*

"Stephenie Meyer meets Jane Austen in this humorous, romantic tale of a girl on a mission to find her very own Edward Cullen. I didn't want it to end!"

—*Mandy Hubbard,*
author of Prada & Prejudice

"We often speak of Jane Austen's satiric wit, her social commentary, her invention of the domestic novel. But Jenni James, in this delicious retelling of Northanger Abbey, casts new light on Austen's genius in portraying relationships and the foibles of human nature--in this case, the projection of our literary fantasies onto our daily experience."

—*M.M. Bennetts, author of May 1812*

Prince Tennyson

"After reading Prince Tennyson, your heart will be warmed, tears will be shed, and loved ones will be more appreciated. Jenni James has written a story that will make you believe in miracles and tender mercies from above."

—*Sheila Staley, Book Reviewer & Writer*

"Divinely inspired, beautifully written—a must read!"

—*Gerald D. Benally,*
author of Premonition (2013)

"Prince Tennyson is a sweet story that will put tears in your eyes and hope in your heart at the same time."

—*Author Shanti Krishnamurty*

Hansel and Gretel

Jenni James

StoneHouse Ink 2013
StoneHouse Ink
Boise ID 83713
http://www.stonehouseink.net

First eBook Edition: 2013
First Paperback Edition: 2013
ISBN: 978-1-62482-058-8

Cover design by Phatpuppy Art
Layout design by Ross Burck

This book was professionally edited by Tristi Pinkston
http://www.tristipinkstonediting.blogspot.com

Published in the United States of America

ALSO BY JENNI JAMES

Jenni James Faerie Tale Collection:
Beauty and the Beast
Sleeping Beauty
Rumplestiltskin
Cinderella
Jack and the Beanstalk
Snow White

The Jane Austen Diaries:
Pride & Popularity
Northanger Alibi
Persuaded
Emmalee
Mansfield Ranch
Sensible & Sensational

Prince Tennyson
Revitalizing Jane

Eternal Realm Series:
Eternity

This book is dedicated to Maralyn.
You always did love candy more than anyone.

Chapter One

THE CHILD'S CRIES WERE loud and strong—strong enough to be heard through the torrential rain and roaring wind. It had been one of the worst summer storms the region had seen in years—breathtakingly horrid. Adale Waithwrite, a simple farmer, hunched down within his thin, saturated coat and wrapped his useless scarf tighter around his head and mouth. Though it was rain and not snow, it was a fierce, biting rain. A rain that was not forgiving or kind.

It brutally pelted his face and hands,

stinging them with every slash of the drops as they flew through the air to cut into his covered flesh. The clouds had come so quickly and forcefully that though it was just past four, you would have believed it to be nigh on midnight, so dark and cold it was.

The farmer heard the shriek again and turned in that direction, skirting the old forest.

"Hello?" he shouted into the sleet and rain. "Hello?"

The answering cries were louder this time and the farmer knew he was very close to the child, who was most likely tucked within the rock crevice. Attempting to climb a large boulder, Adale slipped and banged his knee. No doubt there would be a large bruise in the morning. Mumbling a curse under his breath, the man attempted again to scale the sheer rock, and this time managed to grip well enough to haul his wet body up and onto the ledge. Peering over the other side, he flinched as a great strike of lightning lit up the sky, its jagged lines spearing every which way.

The loud crash of thunder that followed immediately after shook the slick rock wall. When another bolt of light enraged the sky, he looked down and saw the shuddering boy about eight feet below him, right within the crevice as he had assumed.

The boy was drenched, his arms wrapped around himself.

"Come here!" he shouted to the child. "Come! And quickly, too! This lightning is getting dangerously close."

He held out his hand and the boy stood up just as another crash of thunder exploded all around them. "Hurry!" Adale shouted again. "Grab my hand!" Adale's fingers were slipping from bracing himself in such an awkward position upon the boulder. "Now, boy!"

The trembling child clutched his gloved fingers just as the farmer began to slide back down the sheer boulder between them. Another flash of lightning tore through the rain as it poured all around them, and then the bang of the thunder immediately descended. In a show of superhuman strength, he hauled the boy up and over the rock as he slid down.

He balanced the small child against the boulder and continued to slip to his feet. Once he regained his footing, he quickly glided the child the last yard or so into his arms.

The sky boomed and lit again as the farmer ran as fast as he dared in such a downpour. He clutched the boy to his chest and thankfully made it the fifty yards or so into the waiting cottage without mishap. His son met him at the door and stared in great shock at the whimpering child in his arms.

"How did you hear him over this storm?" he asked.

"The Gods, son. They led me to him. They must have." Adale shook his head as he set the boy on the table. "Hansel, will you hang up my coat for me?" He removed his overcoat, handing it to his son. He slipped off his gloves and scarf and tossed them into a bucket near the door. They would need to be wrung out later—his clothes were soaked through. One look at the scared, sopping boy and he knew this would be a rough night.

The child was merely dressed in knee breeches and a simple shirt, with an old wool hat atop his head. His shivers alerted the farmer to the great urgency needed to help him. "Hansel, fetch me a blanket for the lad." His son was quick to place the coat on the peg by the door and run to the bedroom.

Adale pulled the dripping hat off the child and gasped when a long golden braid plopped out, its end tied with a battered green velvet ribbon.

"You are no boy at all, child! You are a girl."

She nodded and looked away, her arms going tighter around her trembling legs.

"Where did you come from? How are you out in a storm like this?"

"I …" The little girl opened her mouth to speak and then her eyes darted to Hansel as he came back in the room, carrying a thick blanket.

"Yes?" asked the farmer as he took the blanket from his son and wrapped it tightly around her. "Who are you? How did you come here?"

Her voice stuttered through her shivers, but Adale finally made it out. "My home—it is gone. Th—they took it."

"Who took it? Who are you? Why was such a small girl left all alone in the woods?"

"Father, let her speak. You ask too many questions at once. Can you not see she is frightened?" Hansel smiled at the girl and asked simply, "Where do you live?"

She took a deep breath and tried again, this time not so unsteadily. "I do not know where it is from here, or I would point it out to you. I became lost." Her voice had a distinct accent.

The farmer hissed and stepped back. "You are from the Larkein kingdom?"

"Yes." She smiled, most likely not realizing what danger she put herself in by uttering such words in this house. "Yes. My father was the king."

"Your father was the—" Hansel gasped and looked at his father. "My word! What have we done?"

"If they knew we had the Larkein princess in this cottage, we would be hanged."

They both looked at the little girl, and her bright blue eyes blinked back at them. She was a very pretty child, and clearly frightened. Hansel asked, "How old are you?"

She put on a brave smile and sat up straighter. "I am six! How are old are you?"

"Ten." He turned toward Adale. "What should we do, Pa? We cannot toss her out, surely. She is too young."

His father stumbled back a few more steps and then slammed his palm forcefully upon the rocking chair. "We cannot keep her here! We cannot! Not with the king's men invading her home this very day. If they knew … if they knew she was with us—"

"What if they never found out?"

His father nearly fell to the wooden floor. "What? Never found out? Are you mad? How can we keep a child—a female child—with a distinct Larkein voice in our home without anyone being the wiser? Hansel, no. I must take her back into the night and allow the Gods to decide what is best to do with her."

"Pa, please! I know they are a wicked kingdom, but please! That does not mean the girl will be too. We can hide her—we can. And she can learn how to speak properly. We will say that she is my cousin, an orphan from your sister Claudine. Everyone knows she has just passed on and left a score of children—they will not think anything of it. Please, Father. You cannot send her out there. She will die."

"It is better that she die than us!" Adale pointed at the girl and she began to cry. "Take her outside this instant."

"No, I will not, for it is not right. She is a child, Father. She can be trained to be good. Let us keep her, please."

Adale walked around and collapsed upon the rocking chair. "My heart is too soft," he muttered into his hand. "It is too soft by far. Now what have we gotten ourselves into?"

"I promise I will take full responsibility for her. I will see that she is safe and teach her our ways. Just do not make her go back out to meet her fate. Perhaps she was meant to come to us. You yourself said it was the Gods who led you to her. It can only be good that she brings."

His father groaned and hunched over in his chair. "I hope you are right, my son. I hope you are right." He threw out his arms. "Fine. She may stay. Though it is with great trepidation I agree to this."

"Thank you, Father." Hansel walked up to the little girl. He peered into her bright eyes and asked, "What is your name? What do they call you in the castle?"

She smiled big then, showing a missing top tooth. "Gretel. My name is Gretel."

Chapter Two

HANSEL WHACKED AT THE tree for about
the hundredth time in the past twenty minutes
or so. Stubborn tree. It should have fallen ages
ago, yet still it remained tall and proud, giving
him the biggest challenge he had faced for
months. He took another wide swing and gave
a shout to accompany the jab as the metal axe
struck the strong trunk.

"Hansel, do not go about killing yourself
over a little tree," commented Gretel as she
approached him with a tall jug of fresh milk.
"Here. Drink. Enjoy. Be calm. 'Tis good for

you." She smiled at his rolling eyes as she handed over the pitcher.

He leaned the axe against the trunk. Gratefully, he took the proffered drink and gulped down rather large mouthfuls of the perfect stuff. Wiping his mouth and then his hand on his shirt, he said, "Why must women be so interfering? Why can you not come out to enjoy the day and hand me a drink without the silliness of believing a little tree like this is causing me commotion?"

She raised an eyebrow and grinned that annoying, superior grin of hers. "I might have believed you had I not come out here just as you shouted down the rafters."

"The rafters? The rafters? My word, woman." He shooed her with his sweaty arm. "Be gone with you. Go fetch some chickens and find yourself in the kitchen where you were meant to be." There, he thought. That ought to get her riled up.

"The kitchen?" Gretel placed her hands on her hips. " As if that is the only place I was bred to be."

Yes, she was riled up all right. Hansel grinned. "What? I thought all women preferred to be one with the fire and to build up the grand feasts for us men. You know, 'tis true it is us who do the dirty work anyway."

Gretel gasped.

He chuckled. "You cannot tell me that what you do in the kitchen is dirtier than what I do out here."

The girl walked toward him, her golden braids glimmering in the sunlight. She had been with them ten years and had grown from a darling child to a very pretty young woman, though Hansel would rather chop off his right arm than tell her so. Her sharp eyes were usually sparkly and bright sky blue when she was happy—now, though, they were crisp and cold.

"Take it back, swine," she hissed at him.

Hansel had been teasing her too much lately, mostly because he liked to see her irritated. It reminded him that they were nearly brother and sister. He needed that reminder sometimes, like the other day when he became angry for no apparent reason as Fidel took her out onto the floor to dance the Sassamer Trot. It was the same dance Hansel had taught her when she was eight years old

and they had danced it together every festival
since. Until Fidel. He grimaced. There was
no basis for his reaction—she should dance
with whomever she pleased. And she should
look at any of the other men in the village and
laugh with them and speak with them and bat
her long blonde lashes at them. Those same
lashes barely concealed the irate gaze behind
them as she glared at him now. He had almost
forgotten what he said this time to get her in
such a mood. Then he remembered. Kitchens,
chickens, and dirt.

Hansel knew as well as she did that
nothing was dirtier than plucking and gutting a
chicken. Nothing. But he refused to take back
his words. No, she should be kept well out of
reach so he would not worry who happened
to like her that day and who did not. It should
be no concern of his whom she chose to dally
with.

"No." He smirked. "I will never take it
back. You are a woman. You are the lesser sex.
It is time you remembered your place around
here."

He did not see the movement, it came
so quickly, but he definitely felt the tug of

the pitcher as it left his hand and the feel of creamy milk being dumped all over his head.

"That, Hansel, is to help you remember that women will always be smarter than men. And you will forever be a foolish boar!" She spun upon her heel and marched back into the cottage.

Hansel grinned through the filmy white substance. He would endlessly pay for her feistiness, but there was something so very satisfying about the fact that she never let him dominate her and continuously put him in his place. If only the other girls in the village would do the same. Then perhaps, maybe, just maybe, one of them would capture his notice.

He sighed and shook out his hair, brushing it this way and that—streams of milk flying everywhere. Picking up his axe, he continued the laborious chore of chopping, this time really putting his back into it. She would forever plague him if he did not get this tree down quickly and begin chopping it into firewood to dry.

His father had chosen this tree so close to the house because he was afraid the next storm would beat it into the attics. Good grief—as

if this tough thing could fall at all. The irony
made him chuckle as he stopped and wiped
the sweat from his brow. He thought of the
past ten years with complacency. He had done
so well hiding the fact that Gretel was truly
a princess—albeit the enemy. There were
days, weeks, months when she would forget
as well. This truly was the only life she could
remember now.

But there was a fire in her—a spark bred
into her that spoke of royalty, of enchantments,
of wealth. He could not quite put his finger
on what, but anyone who spent as much time
with her as he had this past decade would have
known she was of royal blood. Perhaps that
was what drew him to her—the knowledge
that she was royalty.

Nay, it was more than that. There was
something about her that made him fiercely
protective. Now that she had grown older and
become so much more beautiful, he found
it quite distracting as well. She possessed
something none of the other maidens did—an
awareness, a vitality, a loyalty.

He would die for her. Though he would
never let her know that, it was true. It was as

true now as it had been ten years before when he was just a lad, a strong lad who thought he knew all he could possibly know. His pa always said he had an old soul. Mayhap he was right. All Hansel knew was that if any of the guards had gotten wind that Gretel was who she was, he would have faced them—anyone who tried to take her away. He would have faced them until the death.

Still to this day, when someone spoke of the greatness it was to have that enemy kingdom burned to the ground and the royal family hanged, he would choke and imagine his Gretel hanging there beside her parents and siblings. No one knew she existed. No one had tried to claim her back—at least, as far as he could tell.

Gretel used to speak of a family sorceress, and that woman was the only one who would have recognized the girl. She was a witch who claimed to be good, but clearly brought that family to ruin. Gretel spoke of her quite frequently, and Hansel and his father even wondered if the witch had been part of raising the child, perhaps as a nurse or some such. But it would seem she was lost in the fire or hung with the rest of them. She must have been, for she never did come claiming the child for her own.

Not that Hansel would have let her—he had decided years ago that he would destroy anyone who tried to take that girl. Anyone.

The tree cracked and swayed. Finally. With another great whack, he felt it officially give. He stepped back and allowed it to fall with a loud crash onto the ground. Then he sighed. That was probably his problem right there. He could not bear to see Gretel fall. The thought of one of those village lads winning her heart and then dropping her—no, he would sooner face all of Hades than to see her hurt.

He thought of the milk now sticking to his skin and grinned. Unless, of course, it was he who caused the pain—then all would be well.

Chapter Three

GRETEL STORMED INTO THE kitchen and
tossed the empty jug into the water basin. Ooh,
Hansel could be such a menace at times. At
others, he could be quite sweet and endearing.
But it would seem that as soon as he was
halfway decent, he would flip personalities and
become a fool again. She sighed as she washed
her hands and began to prepare the evening
meal. Father would be home soon—he always
came back from the market famished, and so
she would attempt to have the food ready to
be eaten the moment he walked in the door. To

make him wait for his meals would be torture to them all. Heaven knew he liked to be fed, or he would become a grouchy bear.

She chuckled to herself as she began to put together the dough for the meat pies. The filling had been created earlier from meat left simmering in the pot on the stove.

This was a quaint little cottage—definitely not the shabbiest, nor the wealthiest, but just somewhere in between. There was something so snug about it, so welcoming and warm that had always made her feel right at home.

Those first few months—oh, how she had cried. They did not know it, but she did. She tried to find quiet time alone to let her tears fall, usually at night when no one else was awake. Hansel had given up his room and had slept out in the front room until their father had remade the attics into a nice-sized loft and then eventually a bedroom. When she was alone at night, with the scratchy wool blanket they had originally used to dry her, she would curl into a ball and remember the days when she slept on a soft bed in the same room as her sisters and they ate bowls of Larkein candy together, laughing and giggling. She had

missed her family so very much. These days,
the pain was nonexistent, though there were a
few glimmers of memory she had been able to
keep fresh in her mind, especially from her last
night in the castle.

They had all been scared. She remembered
that—it was one of the few memories she had
left of the life she once knew, the day she lost
everything. She remembered the fright that
hung in the air. She remembered her mother
kissing them all and packing up bundles
for them, telling them she would send them
away so they would be safe. She remembered
hugging her father and seeing his fear when
the castle doors swung wide as if she were in
the main room waiting for the invasion, but
that could not be right. Could it?

Gretel cut into the pastry with a knife and
began to add the necessary water to lump it
together for rolling. Why would a child be in
the front room just before an invasion? She
closed her eyes to chase the memories away.
Some things still plagued her, but they were
better off left unsorted.

Adale—her father, as he preferred her
to call him—said the rumors reported that

all her family had been killed. But why was she not? How did she slip away? She had no recollection of getting into the rock crevice where Adale had found her. None at all. And yet, she was there, shivering and soaked through when he saved her.

Thank the graciousness of all good that he managed to find her and keep her. She sighed. She did remember distinctly that he did not want her when he first heard her speak, and she knew it was Hansel who pled for her.

Hansel. She pounded the dough onto the wooden board and began to roll it out. That man deserved to have *two* pitchers of milk poured on him. She might have poured two if it had not been such a chore to milk the cows in the first place. Gretel groaned as she cut the thinned-out dough into squares. It truly was his saving grace, the fact that he had been so kind to her at the beginning and pled for her life. She could forgive him anything when she remembered she was in this lovely place because of him. But there were days, there were certainly days when she wished she could do more than dump milk on him. If he were not so strong and tall, she might very well toss him over her shoulder and throw him into the ravine.

She grinned as she collected spoonfuls of meat and placed them in the center of each square. Then, folding the dough over to form triangles, she pinched the sides closed and set them on the large iron skillet to be baked in the oven. Oh, what a surprise that would be to Hansel to be thrown. She giggled to herself as she set the last triangle on the pan and opened the door of the oven. How she would love to behold his shocked countenance as he went flying over her head down the jagged slope to the river below. It would be worth it to witness the confusion and perfect fright on his features.

The imbecile.

While the meat pies baked in the oven, she fetched a few carrots and began to peel and slice them to serve alongside the pastry.

It was a matter of minutes to get the table situated and the dishes washed once all was ready. She had heard the felled tree crash some time ago and could even now hear Hansel's grunts as the last of the logs were being chopped and stored. He would more than likely be hungry as well. She grinned.

Mayhap she would tell him she had no food for ungrateful wretches today. Being a woman in the kitchen, she was so preoccupied with all her chores that she did not have a spare second to cook something for him.

She checked the oven and saw there were still a few minutes left. It had been such a nice surprise to receive the large iron oven from their neighbors. They were one of the very first families in the whole land to have their own stove. It had been a gift of thanks for all her pa had done for the Andersens while their father was ill that past fall. The oven had come to the Andersens as a sort of inheritance payment from a long-lost uncle, and it had quite set the village on its ear to see the thing rolling in on the huge donkey cart.

Though the Andersens were grateful, they truly did not have room for such a large oven and they felt they should repay her father for all his hard labors in keeping their crops up, which was how Gretel ended up with it. But goodness, was Adale hardheaded about taking it.

Smiling, she untied her apron and hung

it on the peg. She had never known a more
generous man in all her life, and he kept
repeating over and over, "I did not help the
Andersens just so they would give me their
expensive stove. I did it because it was the
right thing to do."

How she loved him. How so very grateful
she was to have such a fine example of a man
in her life. Unlike Hansel. She groaned and
checked the oven again.

This time the pies were ready. Clutching a
cloth, she pulled the skillet out and quickly set
the piping hot pastries on the dinnerware, then
placed the carrots on as well and set the dishes
on the table with a wedge of cheese.

Hansel despised it when she rang
the triangle, so she did it as a last-minute
annoyance while she stood at the front door,
with him not twenty feet away, and banged
upon it loudly with the wand. "Suppertime!
It is suppertime!" she called out as if he were
hundreds of yards away.

Hansel looked up as she first began to beat
upon the thing and rolled his eyes. "Thank
you," he said calmly. "Now my ears may ring
for a good several minutes."

"Oh?" She pretended to pout. "I did not want you to miss your food. All good women need to feed and care for their menfolk." She turned on her heel and laughed as she walked back in the house.

"Do not forget that!" he called to the door as it slammed shut behind her.

She stood on the other side for a moment and seethed. Taking a deep breath, she reminded herself to remain calm when he came in. It would do neither of them any good to be so irate all the time. But honestly, how was she supposed to deal with such a boorish beast? Always needing to have the last word, always undermining her and believing she was something to be mocked and scorned. *One day, one day, Hansel Waithwrite, you are going to regret all your mockery. I may only be sixteen to your superior twenty, but I will clobber you. Wait and see!*

Chapter Four

HANSEL WASHED HIS HEAD, face, neck, and hands at the outside pump as he cleaned up before dinner. The sticky milk had begun to itch and mingle with the sweat in his shirt and hair. The water was so cool and refreshing. He glanced around the yard, and not seeing his father yet, he quickly unbuttoned the shirt and flung it off. Rinsing it in the cold water, he set it aside and leaned his whole torso under the tap and allowed it to cleanse the rest of the horrid stuff off him. Ahhh… this was bliss. There was nothing like cool water after a hot day's work.

He pushed the handle of the pump down and then, picking up his shirt, he shook it for several seconds, allowing the cold water to spray every which way. He walked over to the line and hung the shirt up to dry before clutching one of the sheets Gretel had placed there earlier and wrapping it around his shoulders.

She would more than likely give him grief for ruining her clean laundry. He smirked and hoped it irritated her even more than he imagined as he stepped into the cottage.

Right on cue, Gretel looked up, her jaw dropping, a look of outrage on her face. But just before she was about to utter something, most likely scathing, he explained, "Sorry. I had to wear this—I hope you do not mind overly much. There was a mishap with a jug earlier and I simply could not walk in stinking of sour milk. So I did the only thing I could do—I took off the shirt and borrowed this for now."

Her mouth closed and then opened again. Clutching a wooden spoon, she approached him. "Hansel, if you vex me into doing such silly things, you should not be surprised at the outcome, nor should you—"

"If you continue to act like a child," he interrupted, "and allow your emotions to get the better of you when I am simply pointing out the facts of life, you should not be surprised when someone may need to compromise and use your clean sheets because of your juvenile actions."

She inhaled a large breath, her face reddening to show she was becoming quite the incensed woman.

He raised an eyebrow and grinned. "Yes, Gretel? Is there something you wish to say?"

"Yes!" Bringing the spoon forward, she used it to beat the air and accentuate every word she spoke. "You are the rudest, cruelest, most vain nincompoop who ever lived! You have no decent thoughts for anyone but yourself! You believe that *you* are the only correct one on this earth and you simply do not care about the pain you cause someone else. You do not even begin to see what your own actions do to others. I will not take your bullying. I will not take your uncouth manners and rude ways. I will not take *you*! You,

Hansel Waithwrite, will soon find yourself the loneliest man in the whole kingdom because there is not a girl or woman within sixty miles of this place who would have you!"

Oh, this was too rich. Little Miss Gretel just gave herself away. "Are you saying you have contemplated having me?"

"What?" She looked shocked.

"If you say you will not take me and no one else will, does not that reveal to me that you have thought of such things to begin with?"

She gasped. "Thought of taking you? Of having you? Of all the stupid—"

His grin deepened. "You should be careful what you reveal, for it could very well be turned against you."

"Against me?" She walked closer, this time tapping him with the spoon. "I tell you what a brute you are and how harmful your words are and you construe this to mean that I dream of marrying you?" She shook her head. "Of all the futile things to believe of yourself. Fine. Fine, Hansel. Make whatever your brain wishes to make of my words. I am through speaking to you at all."

"Finally! Peace at last!" He smiled.

"Give me back the sheet first!"

"I thought you were not speaking. Pity."

"I swear upon the moon, Hansel, I will whack you with this ladle. Give me my clean sheet now and go find yourself something else to wear!"

He grabbed her raised arm and pulled her all the way up to him. She pushed against his chest and tried to kick him, but he quickly wrapped his leg around hers, holding her closer to him. "You will learn not to be such a shrew."

"Me?" She yanked, but he held her fast.

"Gretel, I am only holding you here until you stop these mad thoughts of violence. I may be the bane of your existence, but I am not your enemy. And though neither of us prefers the company of the other overly much, I will not allow us to resort to abuse to achieve our most wanted desires."

"The desire to thump you?"

"Yes. That is exactly what we will not do." His eyes traced her worn features. He had not noticed before the worry lines forming upon her brow. Her full mouth was set in a firm line and her normally large eyes were sharp and slanted as she glared at him. Even filled with anger, she was a remarkably pretty young woman.

"There are days when I despise you, Hansel."

He took a deep breath, the faint smell of lavender tickling his nose. "I know. But it is for the best."

"Then let me go."

"Do my words harm you?" he asked.

She looked away, and his gaze followed the long lashes as they caressed her cheek. "Does it matter?"

Yes, it does. "I did not think I was hurting you."

"You did not?" Her blue eyes met his.

"No. I believed you could handle all I threw at you."

She pulled against his arm, and this time he let her go. "I can. Do not mind about such things. You do not hurt me—you will never hurt me. I simply do not care to take your words into account. They mean nothing to me."

He nodded his head and shrugged off the

sheet. Handing it to her, he said, "Here, 'tis yours. You clearly need it more than I do."

Nonplussed, she took the sheet from him. "Thank you," she muttered, watching his mussed brown hair and strong back as he climbed the stairs to the attic room. Slowly she wrapped the cloth around her arms into a messy fold. What had just happened? She looked over to the empty stairs. Why did she feel so terrible now, as if it were she who was in the wrong and not him?

Gretel walked back outside and hung the sheet upon the line, then shook her head. What was she doing? In a great rush of action, she pulled the sheet down, as well as the other dry clothes hanging upon the line. She was happy to see Pa arrive with his cart and horse as she carried her load to the door. "You are back!" she called out to him.

"Yes." He smiled across the way as he maneuvered the horse toward the stables. "Give me about five minutes or so and I will join you for supper. Is Hansel here as well?"

"Aye. He is changing at the moment."

"Good. Good." He clicked his tongue at

the horse and began to pull the wooden cart into the stables. "I have much to share with you both. Be prepared for some wonderful news." He grinned as the cart continued forward.

"What news? What has happened?" Gretel asked as she followed him.

The cart jolted to a halt. "You never can wait a few minutes, can you?"

"No. Never. Tell me, please."

He jumped down, his eyes twinkling into hers. "Very well. I shall give you a hint, mainly because I am too excited to stop myself. Gretel, you are to have a mother! I am to be wed again."

Chapter Five

GRETEL DID NOT SAY a word to Hansel of
Pa's news. She herself was still processing it.
To have a mother, a real mother? Now? Now
would be the most perfect time to have an
older woman in the house, someone who could
teach her those last, final things she would
need to know before she took a husband and
became mistress of her own home.

But then again, what would it be like to
have another woman preparing the meals and
taking over the home duties? What would
Gretel do? Would her stepmother like the way

things were run? There would most likely be several new changes. Several.

It was an announcement that warranted nervousness, but excitement as well.

How wonderful to see her father happy and in love. What a great joy it would be for him to have such a woman in his life. If there were ever a man who deserved great joy, it was he.

Gretel smiled as the men pulled up their chairs and Hansel offered grace. So changes would need to be made, but what was living life if there were not changes?

She was so lost within her own thoughts as the trio began to partake of the food that she barely heard Father explain to Hansel the good news. However, when Hansel asked, "Who is she? Do we know her? What is her name?" Gretel looked up and met Hansel's eyes.

Their father wiped his mouth with his napkin and leaned back in his chair, a sign that he was about to divulge something cautiously. "Well, I am not sure if you know who she is," he said at first. "I believe neither of you have met her. But she is simply lovely, j ust a wonderful woman."

Hansel's brow furrowed and he cleared his throat as he reached for a slice of cheese. "I am very happy you found her. How did you meet?"

Pa was vague as he waved his hand. "Oh, you know, here and there."

"Where is here?" asked Gretel.

Surprisingly, Father slammed his napkin upon the uneaten portion of his food and pushed his chair back from the table. "I do not need you two questioning me. You can be thankful I found someone so lovely to wed."

"I—I am thankful," Gretel rushed to explain. "Forgive us if it came out critically. We are merely curious."

"She is right, Father. We meant no harm; we only wish to celebrate with you and so ask very simple questions, as would anyone. We are delighted you have found happiness."

Adale rose. "No, no. You badger information from me that is none of your business! I have had enough of this conversation."

Gretel and Hansel exchanged glances. Their father had never shown this type of behavior before. It was almost as if he were a new person altogether.

Hansel stood, pushing his chair. "I am sorry you feel that way."

"I *do* feel that way. And there is no reason for either of you to judge me or stick your noses into places they do not belong. I am a grown man. If I choose to marry someone, it is my own decision."

"Yes, Pa," Gretel answered as she also stood. "We wish you every happiness. And I for one am anxious to meet her."

Adale harrumphed before walking away from the table and slamming his bedroom door.

Slowly Hansel and Gretel sat down.

"What was that about?" she asked.

"I do not know. I am not certain what caused his temper to flare up like that."

"It is not like him at all."

"No, for Father is not normally a man who acts as though he is hiding something. Usually, he is quite honest in all his dealings."

"Except when it comes to speaking to people of me." She grinned.

"Yes, well, there is that. Except when it comes to you." He glanced toward the closed door. "You do not suppose something off happened to him, do you?" His voice was lowered.

"Off?"

"Yes, perhaps something not quite on the up-and-up. Something he would wish to hide from us."

"But were we asking anything we should not have asked?"

"No. Nothing."

"Then what could be the cause of such behavior?"

Hansel shrugged. "Perhaps it is her. Perhaps he is embarrassed to tell us what he knows of her, and so he storms out of the room blaming us for our busybody ways when in fact, he is feeling decidedly picked upon because of the guilt he is already feeling within his own heart."

Gretel took a bite of her pie as she contemplated what he had said. Finally she asked, "Do you feel there is something wrong with the woman?"

"What do you mean?" he asked around a mouthful of cheese.

"I do not know." She chewed slowly on

another bite. "There is something about this whole dealing that seems decidedly odd. Have you heard Father mention anything about remarriage before today?"

"No. Have you?"

"I do not believe so, though he has mentioned being lonely from time to time."

"Where do you presume he found a woman? Clearly he has been courting her secretly for some time or he would have never proposed to marry her."

"'Tis funny he never mentioned her before now, do you not think?"

"I do." He placed his fork down and wiped his mouth on his napkin. "You do not deduce they have only just met today?" he asked before shaking his head. "Nay, Pa would never do anything so unwise."

Gretel popped a carrot in her mouth and chewed. "I wonder if that might not be the case. A sort of love-at-first-sight occurrence, which could explain his reasons for not wanting to share the details. He is too amazed by them himself."

Hansel laughed. "You have been reading those silly fairy stories again, have you not?"

"They are not silly."

He rolled his eyes. "Love at first sight. As if such nonsense ever happens."

"I believe it is possible. Why would it not be?"

"No." He shook his head and sat back in his chair, folding his arms. "You are wrong. To fall in love with someone takes years of knowing them, of watching them, of slowly but surely apprehending you cannot live without them and if you tried, your world would never be the same again."

"What a bunch of rabbit's fluff. I look for the day when I will find my true love, when I watch him walking toward me and know—just know—he is the one." She sighed and grinned.

Pushing his chair back further, Hansel went to stand, but sat back down and said, "Why do you females always believe it will be so? As if those fairy stories know anything about life. The only real way a man or woman would fall in love at first sight is if they have been placed under a spell or enchantment of some sort." He did stand up then. "If you wish to find yourself bamboozled by the first fool who hexed you to feel that way, suit yourself.

I for one prefer a real relationship to an instant verve of awareness."

She stood too. "You are all talk, Hansel, and you know it. I cannot wait for the day when you meet the woman of your dreams and she has you fall down upon your rear with folly over her."

Collecting his plate and mug, he carried them to the water basin and then turned around to face her. "Gretel, you are sixteen—sixteen—and already you believe you understand the epitome of love and relationships. I find it deeply ironic that a girl who has never even comprehended her love for another is telling me—a man who has been in love this past year at least—how to go about doing it properly."

Her hand halted in picking up Adale's plate. She nearly dropped it. "You are in love? With whom?"

Chapter Six

HANSEL SIGHED AND PUSHED himself off the basin. "A foolish girl who has no business capturing my heart, and that is all I will say on the subject."

"Certainly you do not mean one of the village maidens?" she asked, amazed she had never heard him speak of such things.

"Of course she lives here in the village. Who else would it be?" He collected the rest of the dishes from the table and placed them in the basin for her.

Gretel was not certain she liked this

conversation. Her mind sifted through several different girls, and she could not imagine him losing his heart to a one of them. "Are you positive you have quite fallen in love?"

He groaned as he walked over to the rocking chair and plopped down. "Yes, though it vexes me exceedingly that I have. I wish a thousand times a day I had not. It makes everything else dashed awkward for me."

"Do I know her?" she asked as she wiped the table down with a wet cloth.

"Good heavens! I told you I will not speak of it anymore. So let us talk of something else."

It was strange to feel her heart grow cold. Why would this upset her at all? She attempted a giggle and teasingly asked, "Oh, so I *do* know her?"

"Gretel, please. Enough."

"Fine. I will allow you your privacy. However, I believe what I enjoy most about this conversation is that you are upset by it." She grinned, genuinely pleased.

"You would find it humorous."

If only it was more humorous and not quite so disconcerting.

IT WAS BOUND TO happen—eventually,
Father got married again. The wedding was a
bit more lavish than one would have expected,
but it was charming nonetheless. Gretel could
tell instantly why he had fallen in love with
the woman. Cora Childress was very beautiful.
Her raven-colored hair contrasted strikingly
against the light summer gown she wore, and
her emerald eyes sparkled under long, thick
lashes. She was a vision of loveliness.

And if Gretel found it odd that Cora had
not come by to meet her and Hansel before the
wedding, she did not mention it to Pa. Instead,
she smiled and helped serve refreshments to
the guests for the whole of the afternoon.

When Cora moved into the house that
evening, things began to change drastically.
Already the atmosphere in the place became
heavier. It was soon discovered, even though
she was beautiful, that Cora was cold and
quick to judge before finding the reasoning
behind things.

A few days after the wedding, she scolded
Gretel severely. "What do you mean when you

say you could not wash the dishes today? This house is a pigpen without them done! I will not have disorder around this kitchen. Do you understand?"

"Yes, ma'am." Gretel bobbed a slight curtsy. "But I could not wash them—"

"Why?" Cora asked, her green eyes flashing fire as she approached the girl. "What excuse do you have for not listening and doing the task I gave unto you?"

"The pump is broken—it sprang a leak. Hansel is outside now looking at the thing, and he specifically asked that I not use the water at the moment."

Cora folded her arms. "So you could not have fetched it from somewhere else?"

"The closest community well is two miles down the road."

"Then I suggest you go immediately."

"But …"

Cora pulled her hand back and slapped Gretel. Hard. "Now!"

"There is no need to strike her," Hansel said as he came into the cottage, wiping his hands upon his trousers. "The pump is fixed. She can simply collect the water as normal."

Cora pointed at Gretel. "Go, then! Get the water at once!"

Gretel scurried past Hansel. They shared a look before Hansel nodded his head to his stepmother and stepped outside.

"Does she hit you often?" he asked.

"Nay." Gretel rubbed her cheek as she walked over to the pump and picked up the bucket.

"Something is not right with her. I do not like it," Hansel said as he followed.

"Yes, but Pa is clearly in love."

Hansel grunted. "I still do not like it." He reached across and took the bucket from her. "Allow me."

"Thank you."

He pumped the lever up and down several times. "Gretel, if she becomes upset with you again, will you tell me, please?"

"Yes."

"She has a very controlling character. She must have things just so. It is not good."

"Well, it is her home now." Gretel touched his forearm. They stood side by side as the water sloshed down. "We should at least try to respect that."

"Yes, but to harm you because she would not see reason does not make it right."

"So you have said." She chuckled. "I am fine, really. With you so worried about my safety, it does quite take away my own need to be concerned over such things."

He set the full bucket upon the ground. When she shut off the pump, he turned and held her shoulders. "Gretel, listen to me. I will worry constantly for your safety. Always. Since the very first time I laid eyes upon you as a drowned waif, I have felt the need to watch over and protect you. I know I have not been the kindest—especially as of late—but I do care. Greatly. And I will not allow someone to use or abuse you. Remember, you are a princess."

"No." She shook her head.

"Yes. You are."

"Hansel, I do not know that life anymore. I am nothing but a village maiden. I work in a cottage. My family is gone."

"No, not my Gretel. You are in hiding—do not cast that knowledge aside. You will one day rule upon your throne. And you will do so honorably."

She gasped, pulled away from him, and tersely whispered, "Shh! I will not. You upset me with this talk. I do not want that life or anything else grand and frightening. I want to be a girl and have a family like all my friends."

He slipped his arm around her shoulder and tugged her farther from the house. "You cannot deny who you are, or what you were born to become. There is a great reason you were saved as you were. Do not just toss this fact away. You have a chance at creating a world that would help many, many more people than just simply a husband and children."

"What of you? What do you wish to become?"

He chuckled, and his eyes met hers. "What am I destined for? Is that what you ask?"

"If you believe this silliness of me, then surely you were destined for wondrous things too."

He laughed. "No, Gretel. My father was a farmer. It is all I will ever become. I will fell trees and fix leaky pumps and raise animals and harvest crops."

Her heart clinched and twisted. Why could she not have such a life? "You will most likely make that village maiden you have your heart set upon very happy, then."

A look of pain slashed across his features. "Not all of us can have what we want."

"What do you mean?"

"Gretel!" Cora's shrill voice interrupted them. "Why are you dallying out here? Get in this house and begin those dishes." She stood by the door, her hand on her trim waist, the feminine pale pink gown she wore shimmering in the sunshine.

"Yes, ma'am," Gretel curtsied and rushed to fetch the pail.

Hansel walked with her and picked up the full bucket before she could. Then without saying a word, he brushed past his stepmother and set the water upon the counter. Gretel came in with him into the kitchen. Her gaze locked with his for a moment as he said, "Remember what I told you." Turning on his heel, he raised an eyebrow at his stepmother and brushed past her again as he walked outside.

"What were you speaking about?" Cora asked as she parted the curtain near the door to watch him walk away.

"Nothing of too much importance." Gretel began to empty the dishes from the basin and plug it up tight.

"Nonsense." Cora flicked the curtain closed. "I know you two believe this is your home, but I want you to consider something, young lady." She walked over to Gretel. "I know you are not Adale's real daughter. And though I cannot get rid of Hansel, do not believe for a moment that I will not toss you out the second it is convenient for me, for I will. I do not need insolence or slothfulness from you. You will earn your keep, or you will have no place to go."

Chapter Seven

GRETEL MADE HER WAY up to her cozy
yellow room and sat down on the small
wooden bench Pa had built for her on her
twelfth birthday, wrapping the yellow-and-
white afghan tightly around her shoulders.
She could handle doing the chores—it was
what she was used to doing anyway. She
could handle the chatter and the organization
and even the constant demands. The woman
wanted to change so many things in the house,
so many things she believed needed to be just
so. She sighed. It was good to see her father

happy and anxious to do all Cora requested—
though she did request so very much.

However, Gretel simply could not abide
her snide comments.

She tucked her knees to her chest and
leaned up against the side of the bench,
looking across the room out the small window.
It faced the branches of the pretty oak tree on
the east side of the home. How she loved that
tree. Memories of climbing all over it with
Hansel cascaded through her mind. She smiled
until harsher, more recent memories took their
place.

She took a deep breath and tried to push
through the pain of Cora's abuse. There were
too many instances. Any time her stepmother
could find fault with her, she would.

"That color does not suit your
complexion."

"You washed those dishes all wrong.
Could you not be taught properly because of
your idiocy?"

"If I spoke with such a voice, I would
never say a word to anyone for fear of
disgusting them."

"This food cannot be edible. Make it

again!"

"Your face and figure are barely passable for one of your age. Oh, well—I guess every village must have a child on the repulsive side so they can celebrate the difference between real beauty and plainness."

"Your disposition is not fooling anyone. You may appear sweet, but the thoughts that roam through your mind can be seen fully upon your features."

"How can Adale and Hansel tolerate having someone so dimwitted and useless in their house for all these years? You clearly should have looked for a new home ages ago."

It would be different if Cora had said these things in front of the men, but she never did. They were meant only for Gretel's ears. She wiped at a few errant tears and took another deep breath. It had just been a few days, and yet she was not sure she could last much longer in such a home as this.

Her shoulders shook. What would she do? Where would she go? It was obvious Cora despised her.

She rested her head upon her knees. Mayhap Cora was right. Perhaps she did not

belong here. She did not belong anywhere.
For a time, it felt as though everything was
going well in her life, but now—now it was all
wrong. However, it was good Cora pointed out
her flaws. She needed to see what to improve
upon. She needed to see what others truly
thought of her.

Ashamed, her face reddened and she
brushed a few more tears from her eyes.
No wonder Hansel could barely speak to
her without arguing. No wonder everything
seemed so difficult. It was her—she was the
cause of the awfulness.

If only she were better and could please
her new stepmother—maybe then all would be
right. She had never felt so alone in this family
before—so, so unwanted.

Suddenly, there was a knock on her door.
"Can I come in?" Hansel asked through the
worn wood.

"Just a moment," she replied as she
dropped the afghan and dashed the silly tears
from her cheeks. Pinching them to help even
out the blotchiness and restore color, she
pasted on a smile and opened the door. "What
do you need?" Gretel stepped back to let him

in.

"Close the door," he whispered. He walked to the little bench where she had been sitting, placing the blanket on her bed. He sat down and waited until she clicked the lock before stating, "I need to tell you something."

"Why up here?"

"They have just retired to their room, so I feel it is the safest time to speak."

"Very well. What is it?" She perched herself on the bed next to him.

Turning toward her, he said earnestly, "I think Cora is planning something."

"I do not understand. What could she be planning?"

"I found an item within her bag this evening. As I came up to my rooms to change, I saw her reticule upon the table in the hallway. I know I should not have peeked, but I did. And I am disturbed greatly by what I found." He paused and ran his fingers through his hair.

She waited.

"Here. The best way to tell you is to show you." He lifted his shirt and reached into his waistband, pulling out a small vial.

"What is that?"

"I have no idea. But it was so very curious, and since it was found within her things, I have been thinking and thinking about it. I believe she is an imposter, a fraud of some sort. She came so very quickly into our lives, and now it would seem as if everything is changing at a rapid pace. And Father has shown no signs—absolutely none—that any of this is wrong. It is as if he has ceased to exist all together and is now only there to do her bidding."

She gasped. "It really is an enchantment, is it not?"

"I do not know. But it would seem that way, yes."

"But why?"

He ran one hand through his hair again, parting it this way and that. "This is the piece I do not understand. Something here does not make sense, and I cannot find the source of such confusion. She wants something, something in this house, and she will stop at nothing to get it. Even marrying Pa."

Was Hansel right? Could all of this be some sort of evil coming to them? "Do you truly believe so?"

"Why else would she choose Adale? If this is indeed an enchantment of some sort." He lifted the dark glass vial and turned it from side to side. The maroon liquid glistened eerily in the light cast from the oil lamp on her dresser.

"How will we know if it is one?"

He shrugged, and then popped the cork off the top of the curved container. Bringing it to his nose, he sniffed slightly and grimaced.

"Does it smell bad?"

"No. It is quite sweet." He sniffed again and made the same face.

She chuckled softly. "Then why do you look like that?"

"Because I am already feeling the effects of the thing."

"What is happening? Is it truly magical?" She leaned closer.

"I do not know what to make of this. It is extremely powerful." He sniffed again. "And it almost smells like… like candy."

Chapter Eight

"LIKE CANDY?" GRETEL ASKED. "Are you sure?"

Hansel brought it to his nose again. "Certainly candy." He pulled away. "It is definitely strong, though."

"What do you feel?"

He groaned and shook his head. "Stuffy, or something. I do not understand. It is almost like being asleep."

"Do you think she is putting Pa to sleep?"

"No. Yes. Maybe. I have no idea. However, I would be very terrified to taste a drop of this liquid." He smelled it again. "Though it is very tempting."

Gretel's chest went cold. "It is?"

He grinned. "Yes, very. I wonder what it would taste like," he said, his words beginning to slur a bit. "I bet it would be very sweet."

She watched in horror as he placed a fingertip over the bottle and turned it upside down. When he brought it upright again, there was a small red drop upon his finger.

"I do not think it is a good idea for you to mess with such a thing."

"I will not taste it; I only wanted to see it." He grinned again. "Have some faith, little one."

"Do not bring it too close. We cannot tell if Pa had one drop or several."

His eyebrows rose. "Good reminder. This is true—we do not know if he is under the enchantment from a single droplet, or if she has continuously poisoned him every day." He held it toward the oil lamp on her dresser. The murky substance seemed almost solid, sitting there upon his fingertip.

"It shimmers in the light, do you see?" she asked as she slipped off the bed and knelt in front of him.

"It is a very pretty potion."

She pulled his hand toward her. "I have never seen one up close before."

Hansel shook his head and asked quietly, "If she has come by this, or created this, what else has she done?"

Gretel's gaze locked with his. "My good, great grief. What has Father got himself into?"

Hansel pulled his hand away and wiped it upon his shirt, quickly stopping the bottle back up. "More importantly, what has she planned to do with him?"

"It makes no sense. What does he have that is of any worth or value?" She held her hand out. "This cottage, while comfortable, is quite simple and quaint. There are a few acres of woodland and good farmland, but at what cost?"

"She does not seem the type of woman who has enjoyed the art of living a simple life."

"No, she does not." Gretel sat back on her heels.

"So what is of worth here? What would be more important and powerful than anything else?"

"It is greatly puzzling."

"'Tis. Though I aim to sort it out as soon as possible."

"It would have to be something that is priceless or unique or—"

Hansel gasped. "You." He reached down and clutched her hands. "It is you, Gretel. It is you she is after!"

"No, you are mistaken."

"Why did I not think of it before?" He stood up and walked a couple of paces away.

"She despises me. She wishes I would leave."

"It is perfect." He smiled and turned toward her. "She must know you are the Larkein princess!"

"You are not listening. She has told me she would force me to leave if I did not do all she has asked." She stood up. "Truly, the woman hates me."

Hansel tilted his head and rubbed his chin. "No…" he said slowly. "No. It is ideal. You do not see. She is forcing you out of the house, away and alone, so she can…"

"She can do what?"

"I do not know, but it must be something grand. Perhaps she is hoping to rebuild the Larkein throne."

"But why would she wish to do that?"

He paced a few steps and then stopped. "Mayhap she is the witch who was involved with the kingdom before. If she knows who you are, we could be in very deep with this one."

"What do we do?"

"I do not know." He paced some more. "Whatever we decide, we must wait and watch first. Gretel—" He spun around. "You must tell me everything that happens in this house while Pa and I are away. Every single word she says to you. You must. Do you understand?"

Gretel nodded. "She has already been saying things." Taking a deep breath, she whispered, "Before you came in, I was contemplating leaving."

"No! You must not. Whatever happens, do not leave this house. Why would you think to do so?"

"She has threatened many times in the past few days to force me away if I do not do this or that. It has become so miserable,

I realize now that I will have to leave. I will have to run and hide in the woods."

"You cannot."

"But what if she demands that I go?"

"If she forces you, then you…" Hansel searched her eyes. "We need a plan. We need to come up with something in case Father or I cannot get to you. We need to be prepared for the worst."

Gretel thought about it for a moment and then asked, "Hansel, what if I left a trail of some sort? Could you find me if I left something upon the ground? Would you come for me?"

"Of course."

"Good. Those woods get awfully dark and a traveler can become lost after a few steps in. I would not wish to be alone for long."

Tugging on her hand, he pulled her gently to his chest, his hand pressing her head onto his shoulder. "I would always come for you. Even if you left me nothing to follow, I would still search and search until I found you."

She sighed, her arms wrapping around his back. She felt so safe right then. "Thank you. I was worried you despised me."

"No." He kissed the top of her head. "No. I have never despised you. I have tried not to like you as much as I do, but I have never loathed you."

"Why?"

"Hush," he murmured near her brow. "I want to discuss this first, while I have you so close. You do ascertain the seriousness of the situation, do you not?"

She snuggled in a bit closer, loving the feel of his broad chest against her cheek. "Pa has been enchanted. She most likely wants me. And will stop at nothing, so you say."

"Not most likely, little one. She *does* want you. She is evil. I believe she is a harm to those she is closest to. Already she has threatened and abused you." His voice became more tense. "Stay alert. Stay calm. Do anything she asks until I can form a better plan about what we must do."

Suddenly Gretel felt numb. She knew she was being irrational, but Hansel was scaring her a bit and her mind could not help it when it jumped from one thing to the next. "You believe she wants the throne, but what if—what if she wants to kill me? What if she wants to get me away from the house so I may die and not be a threat to her?"

His hands tightened around her. "I did not think of that. My word, Gretel, listen to me. We will solve this riddle. We will get our pa back and you will live."

"Thank you," she whispered, loving the tingly feeling of his fingertips brushing lightly across her back. "Thank you."

Chapter Nine

THE NEXT DAY, GRETEL paid particular
attention to Cora and all she did. Hansel had
warned her to act as if she knew nothing, but
that was not quite as easy to do as she would
have liked. Was Cora truly a witch? Did
she really want Gretel dead? Was that vial a
potion, or was this all the imaginings of two
grown children trying to make sense of the
world around them?

Gretel shook her head and chuckled a
bit to herself as she washed up the last of the
dishes. It would serve them both right if all

was fully well in the home and they were merely making mountains out of nothing.

She glanced up as her father shuffled through the door. And it was most definitely a shuffle—a mere shell of the confident man he once was. All was not well. How could she believe otherwise, even for a moment?

"Hello, Pa," she called as he wandered into the kitchen. "Are you hungry? Would you like me to fix something quick?" It was only three, too early for supper.

Adale glanced a moment in her direction. "What did you say?" he asked, his eyes scanning the counter of clean dishes and then the table.

"I asked if you were hungry."

"Hungry?" He looked confused before shaking his head. "No, no, I am not hungry. I am fine." He turned to leave.

"Pa, wait!" His growing lack of appetite was disconcerting.

He continued to walk away as if he did not hear her. She tried again. "Father, what did you need? You came in the kitchen with me. Did you need something?"

He stopped and glanced over before

mumbling, "Nothing. Just Cora. She will help me. You cannot."

She walked forward, clutching his elbow as he began to move again. "Father, please, do not—"

He yanked his arm out of her grasp. "Do not touch me!" he suddenly shouted, acting so very childlike. "Cora says you cannot touch me. Do not!"

Gretel stepped back a few paces, her heart lurching at the fear she saw within him. "I will not harm you."

"No, you will not!" he snarled, fierceness coming out in his surprise anger toward her. "You will not harm me or my wife, or you will know what true pain is!"

She flinched and scurried back until she bumped into the stove. What was happening to him? How much worse would he get? It was almost as if he did not remember her at all.

Adale seemed to be satisfied with her retreat. He smirked and then blinked, his eyes all at once taking on a faraway stare again as he turned and slowly made his way out of the room.

Gretel waited until she heard his bedroom

door shut. She hurried past the living room and out of the house. She needed to speak to Hansel and tell him how much worse Father was getting. They would have to intervene soon, or all would be lost.

As she went around to the back of the cottage, she came flush up to Hansel. "Forgive me!" she gasped. He must have been heading home.

"Yes," he said as his eyes sparkled in the sunlight. "I see how you are—a typical woman, never looking where you are going." He reached out to touch her, but she quickly sidestepped out of his reach.

"Ooh! You will not begin this nonsense about men and women today of all days."

He chuckled. "Whyever should I not?" Looking up toward the sky, he said, "Today seems as fine a day as any."

She placed her hands on her hips. "You *would* believe so! And here I was positive you had become nearly gentlemanly in your manners, but now I see I was most likely mistaken. You are just as big a nuisance as always!"

"Did you come all the way out here to

pick a fight with me, or did you have other things you wish to discuss, my shrewish sister?"

Outraged, she glared at him. There were things she wished to say, of course. But how could she get past his flippant mood to the truth of the matter? With a tilt of her nose upward, she brushed past him, determined to go somewhere and sort her fears out on her own. Who needed to deal with men at a time like this?

She had made it a whole five steps before she felt Hansel's arm on hers.

"Gretel, wait. I apologize."

She was about to push his arm away when she paused and slowly turned toward him. "What did you say?"

"Wait."

"No, after that. What did you say?"

"I apologize." He took a deep breath. "I should treat you better, I know this. But there are times when old habits are hard to break. Please forgive me."

Her jaw dropped. "Hansel?" She searched his gaze.

"Yes?"

"I—thank you."

"You seem so stunned that I would beg your forgiveness." He stepped forward and removed a wisp of hair from her brow. "Have I never done so before?"

"No. Never." She let out a short laugh. "Well, at least not for some time."

He held her shoulder with one hand as the fingers from his other hand leisurely traced her arm up to the other shoulder, and then around her neck to cup her head.

Her skin vibrated with the trail of perfect sparks his touch had created. Biting her lip, she attempted to stop the trembling his nearness caused.

Hansel looked at those lips, and then his eyes met hers once more. "I promise I will do better. Please have patience with me as I learn how to speak to you properly. I am sorry."

It was all too much. He was too close. All at once, everything she thought she believed and knew about him came crashing down in a muddled heap in her mind. This was the Hansel she remembered. This was the Hansel she cared for. This was the Hansel she loved. Gretel quickly pulled out of his arms.

"Thank you," she said as she reminded herself to breathe normally. "I am concerned about Father. He was not acting as he should. It was worse than usual."

Hansel placed his hands behind his back and began to walk toward the great tree some yards away. It was their spot, where they had gone to chat and dream when they were younger. Gretel followed as he said, "Tell me everything. And we will see what can be done."

Chapter Ten

A FEW DAYS LATER, Hansel wiped his
boots upon the metal scraper near the door and
then walked into the house. He shucked off
his wet jacket and hung it upon the peg closest
to the window. It had been quite a rainstorm,
something he had not seen for some time, and
he was grateful to be back within the home.
He tugged off his boots and set them near the
entrance as well. As he looked around the
room, he noticed that Gretel was not standing
in the kitchen as she normally did.

"Gretel?" he called as he padded across

the floor in his wool socks. "Gretel, did you see that storm? It came out of nowhere, and it was as dark as the day we found you."

He paused a moment, glancing around.

The house was eerily still.

Too still.

"Gretel?" he hollered this time, his frantic steps taking him up the wooden staircase to pound upon her door. "Gretel! Are you there?"

"Come in," she called from inside the room.

Relief poured over him. She was here—everything was fine. Taking a few breaths, he willed his heart rate to slow down as he turned the handle and said, "Thank goodness you are all right." The door swung wide. "For a moment I thought something terrible had..."

It was Cora.

"Where is Gretel?" His chest went cold. "Why are you in here?" he asked the woman sitting upon Gretel's bench.

She smiled a smug smile and stretched her legs out in front of her, her bright green skirt arching before her. "Your sister will not need this room anymore, and so I have decided to occupy it."

His hand clenched upon the wooden frame of the door. "What do you mean?"

"I find it is necessary for every woman to have her own room as well as the one she occupies with her husband. It allows for certain freedoms and thinking that would be impossible otherwise."

"Where is Gretel?" he snapped. "I do not care for your reasoning; I want to know where she is!"

"My, my, are not we the agitated elder brother." Cora put a long hand in front of her face. Wiggling her fingers, she admired the immense emerald ring sitting upon one of them.

"Do not toil with me. What have you done with her?"

She sighed before pushing herself up from the bench. Standing in front of him, she placed one hand upon her hip. "I sent her away. It was for the best."

"What? When?"

She shrugged. "Hours ago."

"In the *storm*?"

"Why not? It seemed just as good a time as any other."

A deep, throbbing rage began to pulse through Hansel's system. He did not know whether to strangle her or pounce upon her and rip her to shreds. Taking a deep breath and letting it out slowly, his temper began to mount as he asked, "Why? What is your purpose for removing her from this house?" When she did not respond, his irritation snapped. He banged his hand upon the doorframe and shouted, "Where did you send her? What did you do to her? Does she have a place to stay? Where is she?"

Cora did not even bat an eyelash. "What does it matter?"

"Because she is my sister! And we did not save her life to see you toss her out the second you moved in." He stepped toward her. "Where is my father? I will speak to him at once. You may believe you own this home now, but let me remind you, family is more important than your designs. You will not stand. Father!" he hollered.

"Keep your voice down, boy. He is not here. It is he who drove her to a secluded section of the forest where she will wander for several days until she is ravaged by the wolves."

"You did what?"

She grinned. "The poor girl simply could not do all that was expected of her. She has no reason to live, and I will not have her getting in my way. I anticipate Adale home from this errand any moment now."

"My father would never leave Gretel alone in the forest like that, nor would he take his cart and horse out in such a storm. You must be mad!"

"Interesting, then." She raised one dark eyebrow. "For that is exactly what he did."

Hansel took the last few steps to her. "What did you do to him? He was sane until he met you."

She laughed, a melodiously husky sound, and said, "My dear boy, I did the exact same thing to your father as I did to your sister. And if you do not behave, I will do the same to you as well."

His eyes bore into her emerald gaze. "I would like to see you try!"

Instantly, the door behind him flew shut with a bang. He turned to see if someone had come in, but they were alone. Anger coursed through him like fire. How dare the woman perform magic in front of him? "You are a witch!" he hissed.

She smirked. "And you will soon be a toad if you do not do what I say." She pulled the vial from her pocket and held it out to him.

The enchantment! He snatched it from her grasp.

"Now, would you like to know what really happened to your sister?"

He flinched, hating being a pawn in her game. "I thought you told me she was lost in the forest."

Cora laughed. "Yes, well, I had to make sure I could distract you long enough so I could shut the door. We certainly cannot have you running away."

He stepped back with the vial in his hand to guarantee he had an advantage. "I do not know what sorcery you are about, but I will have you hanged and tried as a witch when this all over."

"Do you know why your little Gretel was taken from the home?"

"If you have something you wish to say, then say it! I will not fulfill whatever

pantomime script you have written in your
head as the puppet or player you expect me to
be. I care for one thing right now, and that is
the safety of my sister."

Flinging her skirts around in a large arch,
she presented her back to him and walked to
the window. "Your foolish temper will see
you killed, boy. I suggest you play the puppet,
or you will lose more than you could ever
imagine."

"Where is she?"

"When you in your idiocy decided to
show her that vial of mine, you became a key
player in this farce. For it is because of your
inane ability to let things alone that I needed to
remove her from this house."

She whirled around, her green eyes
flashing a bright yellow. The long locks of
her raven hair lifted around her head like a
dark halo. Her voice, though soft and barely
above a whisper grated and grinded, sending
the deepest, vilest chills throughout his heart.
Clearly she was livid.

"I will not have my plans upset by a boy
in love with my Gretel!"

Cora stepped forward, her hands reaching

out and curling around the air in front of her.

His throat instantly tightened and he gasped for air.

"Drink it. Drink it all, now, or you will die."

Chapter Eleven

LIGHTNING LIT UP THE rain-filled
sky above them as Gretel leaned over and
pushed the streaming water out of her eyes.
She quickly tied a scrap of fabric to a long
branch as the cart lurched forward through
the pouring rain. They moved slowly up the
overgrown road. Every so often she would
attach another ripped piece of her apron to
the branches reaching out into their path. She
prayed Hansel would find the fabric later.
Thank goodness the rain had slowed them
down as much as it had or she did not think

she would have been able to leave a trail of markers of any kind.

Father had not spoken one word to her from the moment Cora had him pick her up and place her in the cart until now. He simply stared directly ahead and continued to drive leisurely through the storm as if he were in a trance.

"Pa?" she hesitantly asked after a few more minutes. When he did not reply, she tried again. "Pa? Can you hear me?"

Leaning forward, she clutched another long branch and rushed to loop a scrap of fabric around it.

"What are you doing there?"

The shout came as such a surprise, Gretel nearly toppled over the edge. "You startled me." She gasped as she righted herself, pushing off the wooden sides.

Adale pulled on the reins and stopped the horse. "Aye, girl! Get yourself sitting fully in that cart now! No more leaning forward! You are not jumping out that easy! And do not go about tying things to the branches either, you hear me?" He climbed down and walked the few steps over to the branch, yanking off her soggy fabric as he did so. Bringing it to her, he continued to shout through the rain, "If this is how you think to repay me and my wife, then I am done with you! I will make sure you do not tie another piece to any of these branches again."

"What do you mean?" she asked.

He reached down under the cart and removed a large wooden plank from the underside of the seat. "This." His eyes raged a dark, awful color as he approached her, the wind and sleet making him very frightening.

"Pa, wait!" she called out as he raised the plank above him.

"No! No one will find the likes of you ever again! This stops now."

He swung the wooden beam wide and she ducked, but not quickly enough. She felt the sting of the plank as it cracked against her head. Dazed, Gretel slumped to the cart floor, her cheek sloshing in a puddle of rainwater before her eyes drifted shut and she forgot all else.

GRETEL AWOKE WITH A throbbing headache, her back upon something cold and hard. She was not sure where she was, but the smell of candy was strong. It was everywhere, permeating the air. Slowly, she opened one eye to face near blackness before risking a peek with the other. Blinking, she attempted to ease the ache within her head as she cautiously sat up.

It was too dark and too cold to make out much of anything.

She brought her knees to her chest and dropped her head upon them, closing her eyes again. The pain was unbearable. What had happened? Where was she? And more importantly, how did she get here? She could not remember anything. Her last memory was of being at home and preparing for tea.

Groaning, she sat there for some time before she opened one eye again. She blinked until she could focus on the ground below her. It looked to be hard dirt. Perhaps it was stone; it was all a sort of muddled gray. Following the floor with her eyes into the darkened shadows around her, she peered, trying desperately to see what she could not see.

As she lifted her head from her knees, the room began to tilt and spin. It was too much.

It was all too much. She lay back upon the ground and curled her knees into her. This pain must stop.

The wretched smell of sweetness was so overbearing, she was afraid she would be ill soon. And the thought of casting up her accounts upon the ground did not bode well with the megrim she was facing now.

Please do not be sick. Please do not be sick.

She slowly breathed and breathed and breathed until she fell back asleep again.

The next morning was much better for her. At least the pounding in her head seemed to be gone. The smell was not quite as strong, or perhaps she was more used to it. Whatever the reason, she was grateful not to have the overwhelming scent distracting her. She was also very happy to feel the warmth of sunshine upon her skin. She opened her eyes a crack and saw the beams streaming into the place. Waiting for the headache to reappear, she paused a bit before braving the glare and opening her eyes fully.

There was a window right above her, and from the angle of the warm light it would appear to be much closer to seven than her usual waking time of five in the morning.

My goodness. Where was she?

She sat up and looked all around the little cottage she found herself in. It was indeed tiny, a fraction of the size of Adale's home. It was an odd little house, brightly painted and quite lavishly decorated. Vibrant blues, reds, yellows, greens—so many colors pinged and danced their way through her vision. Never before had she seen a place so childlike in its brightness and décor. Was this reality? Was she perhaps dreaming?

She blinked several times before deciding it was indeed real. The layered colors had a distinct sheen to them, glossy and pretty. Slowly she stood and approached one of the multicolored walls. Instead of the gray stones and wood a typical cottage would have, each individual rock seemed to be painted a separate color from its neighbor. Walking closer to inspect the shiny stones, she reached one hand out and was surprised to find a hardened shell-like rock instead of the dense mineral she expected. It was the tiniest bit sticky, not quite fully dry and smooth. This was definitely not paint, but the actual stones themselves were this color.

Looking at her fingers, there were no signs any substance had come off onto them, but it would seem definitely that material would dissolve if completely wet, almost as if it were a food of some sort. Something she would have in the kitchen.

She furrowed her brow. How odd. Why would anyone go through the trouble of building a home if it would not last? It was almost clear as well, as if she could partially see into the colorful stone. Were these an odd type of gemstone, perhaps?

Leaning closer to a bright red one, she was surprised to smell the distinct aroma of cherry. She pulled back. Cherry? That could not be right. She approached the stone once more and sniffed. It was indeed cherry, and it smelled delicious. Almost like—candy. Blinking, she stared at the rock for a very long time.

Who would build a house of candy? Could it be? She stepped forward and this time licked a small part of the stone. It was indeed!

And it was so good. She took another taste and then another. Glancing at the blue stone next to her, she quickly abandoned the red and smelled it. Blueberry!

It was only a moment before she tasted that. Then lemon, raspberry, grape... every different-colored stone did she try. It was truly a magical house.

Glancing around the small, one-roomed cottage, she looked at all the furniture, the slightly tinted windowpanes, the floral centerpieces, the curtains—all of it! It was all candy.

My good, great heavens. How was anyone to resist so much temptation as this? Gretel had never seen the likes of such glorious confections before. And oh, how she truly loved sweets. She had missed them dearly when she first came to Adale and Hansel. They constantly chided her about that sweet tooth of hers. But now, now it was like she was at the castle all over again. Memories of bowls of candy and goodies flooded forth. How wonderful it was then to reach in and take a few of them here or there. The castle had never run out of such treats, and all the children loved dipping their greedy fingers within the bowls.

She giggled a very childlike giggle and

walked toward the small table in the center of
the room. Picking up a licorice whip folded
and twisted into a beautiful flower, she began
to nibble on it. She groaned—this was heaven.
This was perfection. She sat down upon the
only proper place in the room, the actual stone
floor, and began to eat. Fast.

Until that moment, she was not fully
aware of how hungry she had become, or how
much she had missed such wonders. It was
simply bliss.

She chewed and gnawed and devoured
the little flower quite quickly. Not once did
she wonder again how she had gotten to such
a place. Not once did she remember her dear
Hansel and Pa. Not once did she even think
to be homesick. No, this was too much, too
wonderful, too perfect, for Gretel to think of
anything else.

The more she ate, the more immune to her
reality she became.

And the more the enchantment took
hold of her heart and mind and wove its way
through her to capture the great Gretel Elsie
Margaret, Her Royal Highness, the Larkein
princess, would-be queen.

Chapter Twelve

THE WITCH SMILED AS Hansel let out a
yelp when her hands curled around his neck.
This time she loomed above him. This time
she would force the potion down his throat
whether he wished to be drugged or not. The
day before, in Gretel's room, he had thrown
the small bottle against the wall while she used
her witchery to cut off his air supply. Never
again would she be so foolish. Hansel would
pay for that bit of nonsense.

How upset she had become! How livid
once she saw the contents of her precious vial

scattered in droplets and oozing down the yellow wall of Gretel's room. She screeched out a curse and instantly, Hansel had frozen. His arms, legs, neck—all stiff and permanently held in place.

"You will suffer for what you have just done!"she had hissed as she walked toward him. His gaze widened as her snarling face neared. "Yes. You can only move your eyes now, and they are all you will be able to move for some time." She ran her long fingers over his face as she tried to regain some composure. It was not like her to become so very upset. Then again, there were few people actually foolish enough to disobey her. "I suggest you use this time wisely to think over all your actions today, boy, for you are not allowed to treat me and my things with such disrespect. If you do, you shall be destroyed."

She smirked. "I see by your eyes that you wish to do so much more than just stand there and look at me. You wish our roles were reversed, do you not?" She grinned. "Oh, you foolish, foolish boy. If you know me to be a witch, then why tempt your life in toying with me? For do you not know that witches always win in the end? Though you may attempt to thwart our plans, there is greatness in our design that allows for a completion of all our hearts' desires."

Patting his cheek, she continued, one brow rising in disdain. "And do you know what I desire most? Do you? In all your inner thoughts and ponderings over what I could possibly be doing to your family now, have you figured it out?" She stepped back. "Oh, ho! I see by that flash in your eyes that you have. Yes, boy. It is Gretel. Do you know why I want her? Why I would need such a filthy, monstrous, dimwitted thing? No? Should I enlighten you?"

She chuckled and walked slowly around his frozen form. "My, my, my, you do make an awfully interesting statue. Perhaps I will not bother with the potion. Perhaps I shall just place you in my rose garden at the new Larkein castle. Mayhap that would be best. I believe you would set off the tulips to perfection with such an angry stance as that."

Stepping forward and to the side of him, she whispered, "Of course, if I allow you to become a permanent garden ornament, you might be able to see your precious Gretel from time to time."

He looked away from her.

"Hansel, have you sorted out why I would need her? Why I would need the princess back upon her throne, to become the queen she was destined to become? Have you?"

When he glanced back, she said simply, "Freedom."

He blinked.

"Freedom. I want release from this perpetual role of cottage maiden, always living on my own or attempting to blend in with the other villagers. I was made for grander and greater things and I will not be forced into this life any longer. There was a reason I left that girl in your father's care, a reason I chose you two specifically—I knew your soft hearts would keep her safe until the time was right. She is of age now. Sixteen allows her the rights and privileges to the Larkein kingdom and I will not sit back and allow all this time of waiting to go for naught. I need my kingdom rebuilt. I want to live in splendor and beauty again.

"What is that you are attempting to say to

me?" she mocked. "Oh, little Hansel, shall I release your mouth for a moment to hear the words that will no doubt ensure my immediate wrath? Or shall I protect you from your own folly and allow you to stay silent?" She put her hands on her hips, the skirts of the green dress fanning out beneath them. "What shall it be? Two blinks and I will release that confounded mouth of yours. One, I will allow you to stay as happy as you are right now."

He blinked twice.

"Are you certain?"

Two more blinks.

She sighed. "Very well. I shall do as you wish until I am bored of such nonsense." Snapping her fingers, she said, "Release."

Hansel worked his stiff jaw a bit. "Thank you," he muttered.

"You are welcome. Now." She curtsied before his frozen form. "What would you like to say to me?"

"Come here."

"I beg your pardon." She smirked. "Did you honestly command me to come to you?"

"Yes."

Grinning, she took a step forward, shaking

her head slightly. "What are you going to do? Shout in my ears?"

"Come here, please," he said again. "You are a strikingly beautiful woman, and I wish to see you closer."

Throwing her head back, Cora laughed to the ceiling, but decided to humor the poor sap. "Do you not see very many women who look like me, then? You mean to say no one in your village holds a candle to me?"

"Not one. Come closer."

She stepped all the way up to him, their noses nearly touching.

"Release my neck," he whispered.

Cora gasped. Her curiosity about his forward behavior caused her heart to beat quite erratically. There was too much happening. It was too daring—she had to continue. She whispered back, "Release."

His neck inched forward, and Hansel captured the witch's full mouth with his own.

Chapter Thirteen

CORA MOANED AND KISSED Hansel
back.

"Release me," he murmured against her
lips. "Allow me to move about freely."

She did not answer as her mouth explored
his.

Truly, the woman must enjoy kissing.
"Cora, let me put my arms around you and
hold you as we connect this way."

"Release," she muttered into his mouth.

Instantly his arms were free and he
wrapped her up against his chest, his hands

winding around her back, and she melted. This was too easy. Way too easy. He deepened the kiss before pausing for breath and stating, "I would love to hold you as I wish. Help me by releasing my legs as well so I may balance better."

"No."

She pressed her lips to his again and they stayed like that for some time before he attempted once more. "Cora, let me come with you. Let me help you on your quest. There is nothing I desire more than to see the Larkein kingdom returned to my sister. I will be your ally. Let us do this together."

She pulled back and looked at him. Hard. Then she whispered, "Release."

His legs gave way and he immediately stepped free of the stiffness. "Thank you."

"Why?" she asked, folding her arms. "Why do you wish to help me?"

"Was I not clear enough a moment ago?"

"If you make one false move, I will kill you. You do realize that, do you not?" She leaned up and kissed him again.

"Yes."

"And you are not afraid of death?" she

whispered.

"Never."

Pulling back, her eyes skimmed Hansel from head to toe. A grin formed upon her pretty mouth. "Good. You may prove to be very useful. Now follow me." She brushed past him and opened the door.

Hansel turned and watched her walk out of the room. As quickly as possible, he wiped at his mouth and then followed her. His hands shook slightly from the ease it was to outwit her. She was vain, very vain, and as long as she believed him to be infatuated with her, she would be quite easy to manipulate.

He paused at the foot of the stairs when his father opened the door and walked into the cottage. Cora brushed past her husband and out the door without saying a word. Adale looked shattered and lost. His clothing was visibly soaked through and he would most likely catch an illness from the effects of being in such a storm. "Hello, Pa," Hansel murmured as he stepped forward to catch the man's quivering arm. "Let me get you dry." He knew the witch expected him to follow her, but he simply could not leave his father in such a state.

Adale swayed a bit under the pressure of his son's hand, but Hansel was able to remove the worn outer coat and hang the dripping thing on the peg near the door. When he came back to his father, Adale merely blinked at him before asking, "Hansel? Is that you?"

Hansel's jaw twitched. What was the woman doing to this man? How dare she mess with his mind so? "Yes, Pa. It is I, Hansel." He glanced at the open front door and whispered, "Where have you been?"

His father blinked again and stared blankly ahead. "I do not know. I went somewhere far away."

Hansel clutched his arms. "Was Gretel with you?"

Confusion flitted across Adale's features. "Who?"

"Gretel. Your daughter. Remember? Where did you take her?"

He nodded and pulled out of his son's arms. "Nowhere. I did not take her anywhere. It was not Gretel—it was someone else. Someone bad who would hurt us both."

"No, Pa. It was Gretel, and she is not bad.

What did you do to her?"

"I did nothing to her!" Adale snapped. His eyes blazed before settling into a stupor again.

"Then who was in the cart with you?"

"I do not know!" He spun about and stumbled to his chair. Collapsing into it, the poor man began to cough violently. "Leave me be," he gasped. "I did what was best for us. Now leave me be."

"Hansel!" Cora hissed from the doorway. "Stop meddling with things that do not concern you. We must leave at once."

"No. I must take care of my father first."

She laughed, a long cackle. "Your father will be dead in a week—I will make sure of it. Now, if you do not want to lose your life too, I suggest you hurry with me, boy."

Incensed, he stood there for several moments, weighing his options. He still had no idea where Gretel was. His father clearly needed to be warmed and fed and sent to bed—but the idea of Gretel out in the cold somewhere, in the same predicament as his father, pulled and tugged at him. Where was she? How afraid and alone must she be? It was getting late already—the sun had begun to fade. His father would not care for his help, and Cora knew where Gretel was—un less this was all some elaborate hoax to get him away from the house as well.

She clicked her tongue in irritation. "Do not make me regret unfreezing you. I will do so again in a heartbeat if I must. Now come, and you may live to see your sister again."

He stepped toward her. A strange, overwhelming urgency to stay put conflicted with his need to see Gretel. He took another step, and the urgency only increased. What was she planning to do to him if he followed? Or could it be worse—if he left, would his father surely die? "Forgive me. I will go with you as soon as possible, but right now, I must attend my father." He turned his back toward her and walked over to the man.

He heard a hiss and the front door slam shut. "Stand back! You will not touch my husband!"

Adale did not even flinch at the commotion. His glazed eyes stared straight ahead.

"What have you done to him?" Hansel ignored the witch's command and lowered himself to tug off his father's boots.

"If you do not stop this, boy, you will be sorry. Why must you persist in irritating me?"

Hansel slipped off the first boot. "You have not answered me. What are you doing to him? Why is he only a shell of the man he once was?"

"I do not answer to anyone!" she screeched. "Now leave him be or you both will cease to exist this moment!"

Chapter Fourteen

HANSEL PULLED THE BOOT off his father's other foot. He could feel a tingly awareness of Cora as she approached him.

"You would not be so bold as to disobey me," she snarled in response to his defiance.

"Please, I must attend my father. We may leave shortly, I promise. Just let me see that he is comfortable first." His skin began to crawl as she drew even closer to him. He could see the shadow of her form creeping over him, caused by the fading light at the window. Her hands drew upwards and he heard the same

familiar muttering of gibberish she used to
freeze him coming from her lips. Instinctively
he whipped around, one hand snaking out
to clutch at her ankle. Without a moment's
hesitation, he yanked her foot forward while
his other hand pushed against her knee, forcing
the witch to lose her balance and slam to the
ground, her head cracking against the wooden
flooring as she did so.

In just a little over a second, she had been
completely knocked unconscious.

Shaking, Hansel jumped to his feet. What
had he done? He leaned over the prostrate
form of his stepmother and gasped. Was it
truly that easy? Picking up one limp arm,
he allowed it to collapse to the ground. The
overwhelming sense of urgency came again—
but this time it was to run. Now.

As quickly as possible, he urged his father
to take off the rest of his clothes and tucked
him into his night attire, helping him between
the covers of his bed. Then, grabbing a few
essentials from the kitchen, Hansel dashed out
of the house, leaving the powerless witch upon
the floor. Who knew how long she would be
in such a state—who knew how long it would

take to find Gretel. He simply could not wait another moment.

Running into the stables, he saddled his father's horse and took off down the lane. Thank goodness the mud held the tracks of the cart within it. He followed those tracks for several miles before he came to a fork in the dirt road and could not make out which way they had come from. It had grown much too dark.

Was it left or right?

He decided to take the road to the right first. After he had gone several hundred feet, he swung the horse around to try the road on the left. As he was about two hundred feet down the left-hand road, he passed a branch with a piece of cloth stuck to it.

In the now-glowing moonlight, it was easy to make out the pale fabric against the darkened bush. He walked over to it and removed the small piece. Was this Gretel's doing? He retraced his steps to the original road and slowly walked the horse back down it again. Before, his eyes had been trained upon the ground, watching the muddied tracks. This time he looked up. After about eight hundred

yards or so, he was able to make out another
small patch of cloth on a branch.

This one was the same pale color. He
noticed a pattern similar to the apron she
usually wore.

Good girl.

He quickly turned the horse around and
approached the fork again. He cantered down
the left lane, easily following the small pieces
of fabric she had left for him. Every ten
minutes or so, he would come across another
torn remnant.

Thank goodness she had thought to do so.

This went on for a few hours as he rode
his horse deeper and deeper into the woods
and away from any paths he had ever taken
before. In some places, the lane would become
so narrow and shrouded over with trees and
branches looming above him, he would have
to bend down to make it through. How in
the world had Pa made it with the horse and
cart? He was simply amazed. His father must
be locked deeper within Cora's spell than he
originally imagined if the man was willing
to do all this at her bidding. No telling what
shape the cart was in after his jaunt through

the storm.

With Gretel tearing her apron as she had, it was clear she was awake and had enough of her wits about her to remember their little talk earlier—at least that much he could ascertain. He sighed and plowed deeper into the forest, hoping against hope he would come across her soon.

Hansel knew when she had run out of fabric to tear. It had been at least thirty minutes and there had been no sign of cloth anywhere. He finally decided to retrace his steps to see if he had missed a turn in the path or something. He picked his way back up the lane and eventually found the last marker he had seen. Glancing around the dark area, he searched for an opening through the forest that would lead him on. Seeing nothing but foliage, he decided to slip off the horse, tying him to a nearby tree, and go by foot.

"Gretel!" he called out, his voice quickly becoming muffled and lost within the shrubs and trees around him as he clomped through the fallen leaves in the dark. "Gretel, where are you? Can you hear me?"

Everything still smelled damp from

the storm earlier, but the air was clear and the night breeze almost warm. "Gretel!" he attempted again.

Walking slowly back down the lane, he paused every few feet or so to search through the brush for an opening he might have missed while on horseback. An owl hooted nearby and a small woodland creature could be heard scampering across the forest floor behind him. He quickly pushed back some shoulder-high bushes to his right, peering into the darkness to see if he could make out a path. Nothing.

Turning to the left, he was about to do the same on the other side of the lane when he noticed everything around him become still and silent.

It was too still and too silent.

The hairs on the back of his arms stood on end as he listened. "Gretel?" he called, nearly whispering this time.

The sound of the soft crunching of wet leaves reached him before he heard the witch's voice.

"Hansel. So I have found you at last." She laughed and clicked her tongue.

Whipping around, he searched frantically

for her, but she was cloaked within the
dark. He could barely make out the misty
beginnings of the sunrise, but it was still some
minutes away.

"Why must you always make things so
very difficult for yourself, boy?"

Another rustle to his right this time.

"Come here. It is time we settled this once
and for all," she hissed.

Chapter Fifteen

GRETEL PAUSED IN HER munch-munching
of the taffy in her hand. A faint sound broke
through her thoughts again—this time it
was just a bit louder. She took another bite,
forgetting about it until it broke through her
subconscious once more.

She knew that sound. Pulling the candy
away from her mouth, she stood up. What was
it?

Pausing, she waited to hear it again.
"URGHHHH!"
She jumped. This time it was extremely

loud and close by.

What would make such a frightful noise? Dropping the candy to the floor, she rushed to the window, desperately trying to peer through the tinted confection into the woods outside. What was out there? Was it an animal of some kind?

"URGHHH!"

No. She knew that grunt. That was no animal—it was something familiar. Her foggy brain was not working correctly— she could not think at all like she normally did. Something was wrong. Something was very familiar as well, as if she knew, if she could just put her finger on what was really happening to her. But she did not know what to do or say to make the thoughts assemble themselves into some sort of order. Confused, she glanced down and saw the forgotten taffy upon the ground.

Oh, how she loved taffy. She took a step toward it. Already her tongue could taste the deliciousness in her mouth.

"You will not run from me again!" came a shriek less than twenty feet from the cottage.

Gretel jumped again and looked up. She

knew that voice as well. Where was she?
Who was out there? Why did it all sound so
familiar?

"Get back here, boy! I will kill you now!"

"No!" The reply was loud and strong
and so very natural, as if she had heard it a
hundred times before.

Someone was going to die. Gretel stepped
back toward the window to look outside. It
was too marred—she could not see through it.
Frustrated, she walked to the door and set her
ear against it. Did they need help? What was
happening? With her nose so close to the red
door, she began to pick up the faint scent of
strawberry. Hmm… It smelled so good. Just
as she was about to lick the door, she heard
the thundering of feet rushing toward her and
then something slamming into the other side.
She yelped as the whole door rocked under the
impact.

There was scuffling of some kind and
some grunting noises before she heard the
sound of steps making their way around the
back of the cottage.

"Hansel, halt!" yelled the voice.

Hansel. Why did that name sound so very

familiar? Gretel pulled away from the door, this time not glancing at anything particular. Hansel. Who was that? How did she know this name? She rubbed at her face, trying to remind herself of that distant foggy memory, the one that would explain this all.

Placing a couple of fingers in her mouth, she sucked them as she thought. The salty tang of them was an interesting flavor mixed with the sweetness already on her tongue.

She sucked some more, liking the peaceful effect it had on her.

And then she remembered. Just like that.

Hansel! Hansel is being chased by Cora— she is trying to kill him!

Gretel could not remember how she came to be in the strange house, or why, but she knew Hansel was in danger and he needed her. Somehow the salt on her skin counterbalanced whatever was holding her mind hostage.

Her thoughts were less cloudy—now she could think. She had to help Hansel.

Frantically searching around the one-roomed cottage, she looked for any tool she could find that might be of assistance. There was nothing, simply nothing but oodles of edible sweets. Even the chair and table were edible. Bah.

She noticed a small window above the kitchen basin on the other wall. Climbing on the cookie countertop, she attempted to peer through that pane. Ugh. Why must every single surface of the place be candy? Tapping against the solid sugary mass, she could not even manage to get it to crack. Outside, the blurs and shadows told her Hansel was still not caught, but it could not be long before he was. And from the shouting, she knew Cora would soon lose all control.

Frustrated, she slipped off the counter, her eyes taking in the small candy stools near the cookie table. Wait a moment. Walking over to a bright blue stool, she picked the thing up. It was not very heavy, but at the same time it was most definitely not light. It had enough substance in it to do some damage if needed. This would work.

She tucked it under her arm and listened a moment. The main scuffling was happening behind the cottage still. Good. Slowly, she opened the door and stepped into the bright morning sunshine.

Hansel grunted again and dodged to the left. Thank goodness the witch's powers had dimmed somewhat after her fall—he had been evading her for hours and she was still not able to freeze him. One thing was certain—the woman did not give up easily.

He heaved another lungful of air and dashed under the bushes on his right. Exhausted, but not about to give in, he plowed on just a few steps ahead of his stepmother's every movement. "Give up!" he hollered as he felt the bushes next to him shift. He kicked out with his foot and met the solid force of thigh.

She shrieked as she stumbled to the ground. "You will die!"

"Never!" he called back, his feet already scrambling out of the brush into a dead run toward the colorful cottage. If he could get to the strange house, he might find something in there to protect himself and then get his bearings to resume his search for Gretel. Just as he was about to reach the red-and-white wraparound porch, he felt a tug upon his shirt.

No. He was whipped violently backward

and flung upon the ground, landing on a large, sharp rock.

"Enough!" Cora shouted. Her bruised features and shabby, filthy dress rose above him as he winced.

His back ached from the stone she had thrown him upon.

The witch's angry eyes blazed as she loomed over him. This time she planted her knee into his chest as she slammed down on top of him. Hansel groaned and attempted to fling her off, but the grass instantly grew into vines that wrapped themselves around his body and held him prisoner. He tugged and jerked against the pressure of the green straps, but it was all in vain. Within seconds, he was completely held captive by them.

Cora leaned down and grabbed his throat, her fingers tightening and digging into his neck, her other hand slipping into the pocket of her dress. "Now drink this vial!" she roared. "Drink it all! I am through with you—you will pay for what you have put me through!"

Chapter Sixteen

GRETEL CREPT CLOSER TO the pair. Her
arms shook as she held the small stool above
her head. There was no chance she would
allow Cora to take Hansel from her, not after
all the woman had done to destroy her pa.
Hansel grunted and squirmed against the tight
bands around his frame as her stepmother dug
her nails into his throat. But it was the vial—
the small jar of liquid she hovered over his
lips—that lunged Gretel into action.

With the cry of a great hawk, she swooped
down and slammed the stool over Cora's head,

its legs trapping her neck neatly within their framework, her head squeezing between the rungs and supports.

The witch instantly let go of Hansel and screeched.

Gretel shoved against the stool again and the candy chair slid down Cora's shoulders as well. Rolling off Hansel, the witch attempted to rise, but could not get enough leverage with her arms trapped as they were. She teetered and collapsed.

Gretel bent down and yanked and ripped against the green vines holding her brother captive. They would not budge.

"Go!" he shouted. "Get out of here! She will kill you."

"No. I will not leave you."

"Gretel, I swear in all of God's good grace, you must leave this place now. I have been searching for you all night—now that I know you are safe, you must leave."

"No. I will not run off with you in such a state."

Cora laughed. "You two children will cease your bickering," she muttered into the ground where she remained. "It tires me."

"Gretel," Hansel hissed as she continued to pull and tug at the vines trapping him. "Neither she nor I can move right now. You must go. You must."

"It does no good to speak to me of this. I will not leave you here." She glanced to the right of him and under his shoulders, attempting to see what held the vines in place. "Is this grass? What sorcery is this?"

"Yes, you fool!" Cora snarled. "Everything around this cottage is under an enchantment, can you not tell? Or are you too daft to figure this out for yourself?"

"Do not speak to her that way!" Hansel grunted and jolted against the strands. "You will regret every word spoken."

"Shh… Do not antagonize her." Gretel tried to free him. Still nothing. She glanced around, seeing if there was anything she could use to cut the strands. Spying the vial laying on its side upon on the ground a few feet away, she snatched it up.

"Do not touch that!" Cora shouted. "Put it back! Put it back now!"

The grass began to tremble beneath Gretel and she opened the small jar of liquid as the green blades grew into vines, winding themselves around her feet and legs. Not sure what to do, she placed a small drop of the liquid upon one of the strands that held Hansel prisoner. It instantly sizzled and recoiled— evaporating before her eyes.

"Did you see that?" she asked, the strong vines tightening around her legs.

"Yes! Do it again."

She dripped tiny droplets of the potion over several of the cords both on him and the cords on herself. They all recoiled and shrank into grass again. Within moments, Hansel was free.

"You are brilliant!" he exclaimed, his arms wrapping around her as he pulled them both up. "What made you think to use it?"

"I have no idea. It was the only thing I had—I am just grateful it worked."

"You two may rejoice now, but you will not be alive long enough to enjoy it."

"Strong words for a woman who is caught up and facing the ground at the moment." Hansel walked over to her. Cora did not flinch. "What were you planning to do to our father?"

"The same thing I will do to both of you."

She grinned into the dirt and then coughed a bit. "Make you sweet enough to eat, of course."

"What? You were going to eat us all? Are you mad? What of Gretel becoming the Larkein queen?"

The witch cackled before sputtering into coughs again. "Do you honestly believe I would have captured her to put her on the throne? Are you seriously foolish as all that?" Her foot pushed against his leg, allowing her to turn over to see him better. "No. She was just going to be the last one of you I ate. I always take on the appearance of my most recent dinner." She grinned. "Poor Cora Childress did not know what was happening to her when she became captivated by my candy."

"You *ate* her?" Gretel thought she was going to be sick. She swayed slightly and walked toward the red-and-white-striped pillar of the porch a few feet away. Setting one hand upon it to steady herself, she asked, "Why me last? I do not understand."

Hansel interrupted the witch. "So she could tell the world she was you and they would all believe it, allowing her to become—"

"Allowing me to become Queen Gretel."

"But why?"

"Why?" the witch shrieked. "Why? You fool! So I can rule and reign in such a state forever!"

"So you brought me here to be eaten?"

"Yes, to sweeten you up and keep your mind so foggy that once I was through with you, I would be able to partake of your sugariness."

All at once, the candy Gretel had eaten seemed to churn and bubble within her stomach. It hurt. All of it cramped and stirred inside.

"How did Gretel break free?" Hansel walked over to his sister and collected the vial she held while asking, "Clearly she is not under the mental fog you thought she would be—though she does not look well. Gretel, how are you feeling?"

"I am going to be ill."

Just then she groaned, and they both watched as Gretel ran from them to a nearby bush and began to spew out the candy.

The witch sneered as the girl heaved and heaved. "Salt. She must have gotten into some. It is the only antidote."

"Do you have any salt upon your person?" he asked as he approached the witch again.

"Of course not!" she snarled. "Do you think I wish to offset all I have worked toward? Absurdity does not become you."

He knelt upon one knee and leaned over her. "Though we have shared a few kisses, I feel it is wise to tell you, I do not believe it would ever work between us."

She hissed at him and attempted to lunge forward.

"Now, now, do not worry. I can see you are as eager to be rid of me as I am to be out of your presence. So I feel this is honestly the only thing I can do at the moment." He unstopped the vial.

"You would not dare!" Her eyes flashed with rage.

He grasped her jaw with his strong hand and poured a great amount of the poison down her throat as she coughed and sputtered. "I am afraid I already have." He smirked.

Chapter Seventeen

AS GRETEL CAME BACK, her stomach more settled, she was surprised to see Hansel dragging the witch across the ground and up to the house. "What happened?"

The beautiful, fiery woman was now a sputtering simpleton. She did not complain one bit as he pulled her by her trapped shoulders and heaved her onto the candied porch. "Get the door for me," Hansel called out.

"Why is she like this? What did you do?" Gretel rushed past him to open the door.

"Just gave her a taste of her own magic." He grunted a bit as he hauled Cora's limp body up to be tossed upon the floor inside the house. He then broke off several flowers from a vase on the table and placed them near her eager mouth. She began to nibble at them immediately.

"The vial?"

"Aye."

"You did not! You actually gave it to her?" She chuckled.

"Well, what else were we supposed to do with the woman? She would eat us otherwise. So I guaranteed she would remain in the same stupor she was willing to inflict upon us."

Gretel laughed again and shook her head. "I would never have thought to do so. You are quite wonderful—you know that, right?"

He grinned and shrugged. "It took you long enough to notice."

"What?"

Hansel walked over to her and looking down, nudged her with his elbow. "Come—admit you noticed my charms before now."

Giggling, she rolled her eyes. "Never. I will never admit to believing you are anything but a nuisance!"

"Yes, yes, I know. I am the typical awful big brother." He tugged one of her braids, his eyes going serious all of a sudden. "Though I am grateful to find you alive. You gave me quite the fright."

She stepped into his chest and wrapped her arms all the way around him. "Thank you for looking all night for me," she murmured into his dirty shirt.

"I would have looked longer, little one. I would never have stopped looking for you."

She nodded and sighed. "Thank you. What would I have done without you?"

He coughed as if he were embarrassed, the great sound resonating through his whole form. "Was it not you who saved me in the end?"

"Yes, but only because you came all the way to me."

"I love you, Gretel."

Her heart jolted until she realized what he was truly saying. "Aye. I know. I love you and Pa so very much."

He gently pulled her away from him and looked right into her eyes. "No, I love you more than that, dear. I love you. It is *you* I have been in love with all along."

She was not sure she could breathe. Did she hear him right? Was it truly her? "Hansel?"

"I know you are young. I know it is probably not the time to even whisper such things to you. But I have had these thoughts for some time now, and if I do not say them, I may burst. Or regret it for the rest of my life."

He was the most wonderful man in all the world. "Hansel!" She caught him up tight. "I love you. I love you. I have always loved you."

"Are you sure?"

Another surprised chuckle burst forth. "How could I not? My dearest Hansel, you have been the only one to see me and love me from the first moment we met. If not for you, I would surely have died in that storm. You cared for me when no one else thought to do so. I owe you my life. I owe you everything."

"What you owe is the privilege of seeing you settled upon the throne that is really yours. That will be all the payment I deserve or could ever want." One hand ran up her back, leaving a delicious trail of sparks.

She shook her head. "No, I will not go there. I do not wish to go there ever again. That is not the life I choose for myself—it never will be. That life is gone now."

"You do not know what you say. Our king does not deserve the Larkein kingdom. You do. You surely cannot mean to give up all your rights and privileges now? Not after all that has been done to take care of you and bring you up."

She pushed away from him. "What privileges? What rights? I have heard the gossip in the village! I know that my kingdom was a wicked, cruel place. What right have I to take it back now? None. My rights, my glories, they all rest and lie upon this *right* here, right now: the fact that I am allowed a second chance—nay, a third chance; the fact that I am alive and thriving and growing and happy. Hansel, I am so happy. You do not speak of a life with you. You speak of a life with me as a queen ruling a kingdom my family does not deserve—*I* do not deserve. I want a small cottage in the woods, raising a gaggle of children and loving my family every day. I do not want the invasions, the politics, the outrage, the horror... no, my dear Hansel, I just want you."

She clutched his hands. "Please do not make me face a life I was never destined for. Please accept that I am truly much happier here and I always will be."

"But you are a queen."

"No!" Dropping his hands, she turned away from the silly witch upon the ground and leaned her head against the doorframe. She closed her eyes and whimpered. "Must we continuously go round and round over this? Must we? What will make you see reason? Is there anything?"

"Will you allow me to take you to the Larkein castle before you make your decision?"

She sighed, knowing there was no hope for his madness. "Yes, if you must. I will attend you and visit my old home." Holding out one hand, she exclaimed, "I will promise to consider all my options carefully, but no matter what I decide, I would that you allow me the right to govern myself." Grinning, she finished the rest. "For if you truly believe I am queen, then remember, I am also of a right

and rank to do as I see fit without the help of a
meddling village lad!"

Chapter Eighteen

HANSEL CHUCKLED AS HE walked to the door. "Come. We shall go as soon as we take care of the witch."

"What do you plan to do to her?" Gretel asked.

"The only thing we can do at this moment is to guarantee that no one else will be made to suffer because of her again."

"You mean to *kill* her?"

"I mean to burn her to ensure that she never comes back again—in any form."

Gretel gasped. "How?"

He pulled her out of the doorway and glanced back in at the trapped witch, happily gnawing away at the stool holding her captive. "She is so engrossed in eating, she will not even feel the fire lapping at her feet. And she will be in flames long before she is even aware of what is happening." He closed the door and pulled out a small piece of flint and steel from his pocket folded within a cloth casing. "Step back."

Gretel climbed off the porch and stood a few feet away from the cottage. She watched as he struck the steel to the flint several times against the bottom of the wooden beams supporting the candied door until it began to spark and then eventually light. The fire crawled its way quickly up the door, its flames licking wildly at the melting candy. Within moments, the door dissolved into a flaming puddle and the fire rapidly spread to the outer casing of the cottage and then within.

"Hurry." Hansel jumped off the porch and ran to her, grabbing her hand. He turned and pulled her through the woods to a safer spot some ways away. Already, the whole candied cottage was alight. "Would you like to stay and watch?"

Her heart lurched as her gaze scanned the inferno. "No, please. I would rather not."

"Very well. Let me try to find our way back to Father's horse and I will get you to safety."

"Will the rest of the forest be all right?" she asked, glancing back as he pulled her through the thicket. What if it all burnt down? "Wait." She paused a moment, and Hansel stopped with her.

"It should be fine. There is a large clearing around the cottage, and with the whole thing being made of sugar, it will simply melt and dissolve without too much mishap."

Taking a deep breath to calm her nerves, she said, "It smells so divine. Even from here."

"Yes. It does. Almost as if we were baking a pie of some sort and not a witch at all."

Gretel frowned. "It is like she is in her own oven."

He wrapped his arm around her shoulders. "Do not overly worry yourself. She was wicked—pure evil. If we had not done what we did, think of who else she would have destroyed. *And* she never would have rested until she had eaten you."

She shuddered.

"I would not have allowed it to happen. Do not fret—all is as it should be."

"Thank you." She smiled a sad smile, and then, lightening the mood, said, "Yes, but it does make me awfully hungry."

"Then let us go and find something to eat. However, I believe we are not too far off from your castle."

Groaning, she tilted her head and rested it upon his shoulder, loving the feel of his arms as they wrapped her up tighter. "I did promise to visit it, did I not? But does it have to be quite so soon?"

"Well, since I believe we have wandered into your kingdom, it is on our way home. That is, if the spires I made out this morning while running from our stepmother belonged to your castle. At the very least, it does deserve our respect in visiting the place."

She rolled her eyes and snuggled in closer. "Only if you can promise me supper—a decent meal—without anything sweet in it. Then I may actually consider stopping by."

He chuckled and kissed her brow. "Done.

We shall go at once."

By the time Hansel and Gretel had made it to the horse and then rode the beast together to the nearest inn, it was well past dinnertime. He paid for their meal and separate clean bedrooms and allowed for a good night's sleep before venturing out toward the castle. The innkeeper had assured them it was just a mile or two up the lane.

Hansel thought he heard him mutter, "Though why anyone would wish to go there is beyond me," but he was not sure, and did not wish to open that discussion. Instead, he waited until the morning and then, renting a second horse from the inn, he and Gretel took off after a hearty breakfast.

As they picked their way to the top of the mountain where the fortress once stood, he could tell before the whole thing had come into view that this was most definitely not an inhabitable place anymore. There were hardly any bricks left, apart from a couple of lonely spires. It was quite simply torn down and only a few fragmented ruins remained.

"Where did it go?" she asked as she got

off her horse.

Hansel got off his horse as well. "It would seem the villagers decided to make use of the strong bricks and mortar within their own homes and lands. It is what most likely makes up the rows and rows of brick fence we passed by earlier."

Gretel began to chuckle, and then a hearty laugh accompanied her after a few moments. Relief poured from her in droves, a giddy release indeed. And it was good to feel so carefree and jolly—it had been too long since she had felt this much joy.

"Well, I guess there is no real reason to be here, is there?" Hansel chuckled with her as he joined in after a few minutes.

She crossed over to him and wrapped her arms around his waist. "I hoped you had an actual castle in mind when you thought of me living here." She grinned and bit her bottom lip to hold in check another bout of the giggles.

"Very well. You win. You do not have to be a queen in the Larkein kingdom after all."

Smiling, she said, "Thank you. Now can we go home?"

"Yes."

He leaned down and kissed her happy mouth quite thoroughly, causing her heart to flutter all the more. After some time he pulled back and said, "Was that witch really hoping to live in this heap? Or do you think she would have rebuilt the thing?"

"Hush. I have waited too long to kiss you," she said. "Let us never think of her again. There are so many more enjoyable things to do at the moment."

He laughed, his eyes sparkling down at her. "You know, this may be the first time it has ever happened, but I believe you are correct." And then he quickly stopped her outraged gasp with another heart-melting, knee-buckling kiss until she forgot all else but how wonderful it was to be in his arms.

Sometime later, as they were preparing to leave, he said, "Once home, we need to get some salt into Pa so he can come back to us."

She stepped toward him, focusing on his handsome grin. "Salt?"

"I will tell you as we ride. But first, I think I need another kiss."

She gladly raised her mouth to his.

Chapter Nineteen

AFTER THEY MADE IT home, it was only a matter of a few hours to get Adale back in order and his mind fully functioning. He had been given such strong doses and was kept on such a continual need for more that they later found a drawer full of little vials for him to take while they were away. The witch had definitely thought of every detail.

Hansel and Gretel continued to stay in the cottage and look after him. It was nearly two more years before Adale noticed the blooming attraction between them, so oblivious to the

idea was he. But once it was made known,
it was only a matter of weeks before he had
the couple married off and settled into the
neighboring cottage Hansel had built some
months before for himself, but never truly
used since he was apt more often than not to
be found in Gretel's company, helping her
in any which way she needed or desired—or
arguing with her, of course.

They lived a very happy, simple life,
something she glorified in doing. It was a
dream of hers to have children, and so, when
Jack was born and then Jill a few years later,
she was thrilled beyond measure.

They were happy, precocious children,
spending many hours exploring the woods and
climbing all over the countryside looking for
adventure. Hansel and Gretel taught them all
they knew, allowing them to become quite fine
adventure seekers in their own right. And of
course, they made sure to relay the tale of the
cunning witch who nearly ate them all.

Later in life, when Jill and Jack were
nearly grown, Hansel and Gretel were given an
opportunity to adopt an infant. Hansel looked
into Gretel's eyes and there was no hesitation.

They said "Yes!" instantly, and then grinned to have found they were of the same mind.

Little Verity grew to be a beautiful young woman who captured the hearts of many of the village lads with her long, dark hair and rosy complexion, but she had the temperament of her loving mother and father and eventually settled down with a simple farmer like her pa to raise her own family like her ma.

And that is how the tale of Hansel and Gretel came to be—one Larkein princess who found herself quite distressingly on the grounds of the enemy, and a brave young farm boy who did all in his power to guarantee her safety.

With such a beginning, how could they not be destined for a happily ever after?

THE END

Jack and the Beanstalk

CHAPTER ONE

"WHAT DO YOU MEAN, she is gone?" Jack asked as he whirled around on his heel, his great brown overcoat flinging about with him. "What has been done to bring her back? Has anyone even attempted to call the authorities?"

The old woman wrung her hands nervously over her pump form. "We have! There was nothing they could do. We sent for you as soon as possible."

Jack paused his pacing on the worn rug in

the main cottage room of his dearest Rachel's
home. "So you mean to tell me that sometime
last night, Miss Rachel, *my* Miss Rachel, was
taken forcefully from her bedchamber by a
great beast of a man, and none of you bothered
to wake me up to attend this search of her?"
He was livid. He was *more* than livid. He
was terrified, heartbroken, worried out of his
mind. "Why, it is nearly seven o'clock in the
morning! This giant monster is hours ahead of
us, and I am just now hearing of it."

"We are sorry!" cried the man Jack had
hoped to call a father one day. "We were not
attending properly. All we could hear ringing
in our minds was the memory of her screams
of fright over and over again as he took her
from us."

Jack was going to be sick. He swallowed
and breathed deeply before attempting to
speak again. "I understand this house has been
under great duress the past few hours, but you
must know I love your daughter more than I
love my own life. I am frantic with the need
to rescue her at this moment. Please, I ask
that you forgive my hastiness in chastising
you at such a time and instead, give me any

bit of information you can so I may bring my fiancée back. Anything at all." He knelt before the older man and woman, still in their night attire with shawls and slippers. " And I vow to you both that I will not give up my search for your daughter, unlike the authorities. I will not simply hear who has captured her and run in fear. Nay, I am yours, I am hers, and you *will* see her again or I will die trying to attempt the thing."

"Oh, Jack! What would we do without you?" Mrs. Staheli clutched his hands, tugging him up. "Come and have a cup of tea and we will tell you all we know."

He shook his head. "No. I would prefer to hear it all now, just as we are, so I may begin this search instantly."

"Son, it is useless. The monster—the giant—he took her up in the clouds," her father answered as he ran his hands through his hair.

"I beg your pardon—he took her where? No, wait. Start at the beginning and tell me everything you can of this giant and all that happened. I will see what is to be done."

Celeste glanced over and shared a look

with Hans.

Jack leaned toward the couple and tried his best not to let his growing irritation show upon his face as Hans cleared his throat. Why were these two moving so slowly? Every second wasted was a second he could be using to fetch Rachel back.

"It was quite late—nearly morning—when he came," Hans started.

"Yes, I know this. Why did he abduct her? Did he say?"

Celeste clutched her shawl. "Yes! Yes, that is definitely something I can answer. He wanted her voice. Apparently, his ears picked up the sound of her humming and singing the other day while she was in the meadow picking those flowers." She pointed over to a vase of wildflowers on the worn oak dining table. "He decided to bring her back to his castle so she would sing for him."

"And he also mentioned something about her playing the harp for him," Hans added.

"The harp?" Jack tried not to smile at the absurdity. "She does not do any such thing."

"So she told the giant." Hans folded his arms. "But he would not listen to her."

"Why did he not take her when he had her alone in the meadow?" Jack asked.

"He did not say."

"How did he get here? And you are certain he took her up to the sky?"

"Aye." Hans unfolded his arms and then clasped his hands together. Jack noticed the slight tremor as Celeste hung on to her husband's elbow. "We heard her shouts for help and came in the room immediately. The giant's huge head peered into the windows. One long arm snaked in and captured her up in his palm. She tried to make him see reason and not take her from the house. I believe he is a bit dimwitted, as each time Rachel asked him a question, it slowed him down—he would stop and think about it and then answer her. It was a clever ploy and even we joined in until he caught on to what we were doing. Then he swung his arm out and brushed us both down before wrapping his fingers around her and sliding his hand through the window again. It was a tight fit and required precision to get his fist out."

"What are some of the things he said?"

"Most of it you already know, like the fact

that he was taking her up to his kingdom in the clouds where she was meant to live in a golden cage and sing for him, or play the harp. And how he had found her in the first place."

"How did he get back up to his kingdom, and where did he come from? Has anyone heard of this giant before?"

"We had no idea he existed until he came for her." Celeste brought her hand to her mouth. "So, so terrifying."

"This is all baffling. No wonder the authorities are useless. Where does one begin? How does one get all the way up into the clouds to rescue her?"

Hans pulled away from his wife. "If you follow me outside, I can show you his tracks and where they lead. When we made it to the window and watched him take her away, it was as if the giant were climbing on something, but we could not make out what it was. Indeed, there was nothing to be seen there at all."

"It was all so odd and confusing, and her cries could be heard for a long while in the still of the night. It was just too distressing for words," Celeste added, her voice shaking.

Jack patted her hand and then nodded to Hans. "Let me follow you where the tracks lead. Perhaps I will find something then, something to make sense of this all."

Hans paused at the door as he pulled on his outer coat. "Celeste, we will be back shortly."

She shooed them away with her hand. "Yes, go. I could not bear to go out there again anyhow."

As the men stepped outside, Jack was amazed to see that the giant's footprints had formed twenty-foot craters all over the Stahelis' garden as well as the road and up a small embankment about a half mile away. They did not need to travel that far to see the great indents he left.

"Are you sure that is where they stop, up there?" Jack pointed to the hill.

"Yes." Hans turned and gestured toward the cottage. "And from that window just there—her bedroom window—is how we watched him make his way up an invisible rope or ladder of some sort, clear up into the clouds until they could not be seen anymore."

Jack placed his hands on his hips and

shook his head, his eyes scanning the sky above them.

His father and mother, Hansel and Gretel, had warned him that life was full of adventures and one day he would meet one that would change everything he had ever believed about himself. He sucked in a long breath of air. It would seem his particular adventure had met him after all.

There was a certain giant out there who needed to be introduced to the wrath of Jack.

ABOUT THE AUTHOR

JENNI JAMES IS THE busy mom of seven
rambunctious children ranging from the
ages of 2 to 16. When she isn't chasing them
around her house in sunny New Mexico, she is
dreaming of new books to write. She loves to
hear from her readers and can be contacted at
jenni@authorjennijames.com or by writing to:

    Jenni James
    PO Box 514
    Farmington, NM 87499

Printed in Great Britain
by Amazon.co.uk, Ltd.,
Marston Gate.